also by Devon Attaei

I Can't Sleep
Fresh Air & Lilac Perfume (coming 2021)
Five Years Without You (coming 2021)

for the man who inspired the first chapter of this novel...

(Please note that this novel contains graphic depictions of domestic violence as one of its main themes)

ON
TO
THE
NEXT
ONE

Prologue
2016

The blue and red lights are swirling all around me. For a minute, while I try and calm myself, I count the amount of times the electric blue flashes across my eyes, "sixty one, sixty two, sixty three, sixty-"

I'm interrupted by a black baton tapping softly on the glass window. I just realized that I'm speaking out loud.

"I usually ask people to wait till we get to the station to place their call, but you seem young... Do you have someone who could meet us there?" the officer asks me.

When he says this, my mind goes blank; I cut everyone off months ago. I'd rather go to jail with a bloodied nose and a torn-up dress than tell him that. The only person I can think to call, was the person who put me in this situation. They can't identify who I am and I don't have my I.D. or my phone. It's probably for the best, right now.

I shake my head "no".

"I'm just trying to help you," he pleads with me. I'm not sure why he even cares.

The fact that my life has even gotten to this point has me feeling lost. I ignore him, still shaking in disbelief, disoriented. I feel like I'm high. He looks at me, trying to meet my eyes, but I already have my head rested on the window and I'm looking in the opposite direction trying to feel something. This numbness is depressing me further than I knew to be possible. He shakes his head while tapping the roof of the car to signal the officer in the front seat to take me away. He picks up his radio and makes a call into the station. I don't know what any of his words mean, I don't care enough to decode them. The lights of this familiar town fill my eyes and I focus on them as we speed by. They dance past me, taunting me. I don't know this place at all anymore.

The silence of the backroad at night calms me. My shakiness stills as I prepare for what's to come. The officer has both of the front windows down. The air rushes into the car and sneaks through a crack in the glass barrier that is separating myself from the officer. It wraps tightly around my flushed face. I soak it in knowing that this will probably be one of the last times I feel fresh air for a while.

The blood on my face is drying. I forget it's even there until I rub my finger against my cheek. A piece of it cracks off and floats onto my lap. I look down at my green dress. There's so much blood that my stomach knots at the sight. As we pull into the station, I immediately recognize it. "The Old Don Jail" the sign reads. Shit. I've been here before. That recollection alone causes my eyes water.

"How could I let this happen," I mouth. I don't know if any sound comes from it. I know exactly how this happened. I knew from the moment I met him that this is where I'd end up.

Chapter One
2010

"Do you think this skirt is too short?" I ask Alex while tugging at the ends to somehow stretch it longer.

"Yes," she says letting out a laugh. "If you bend over at any point of the night you'll catch stares from every guy in the room. And not in a good way." She tosses me a red dress. "Try this," she calls out.

I roll my eyes and walk back into my closet, ripping the skirt off and replacing it with the outfit Alex has just given me. The straps perfectly drape around my shoulders and cut into a low "V" shape behind my back. It looks great. I hate to admit that she's right, yet again.

"You look hot. That's the outfit," she says with pride. "Now let's go. The cab is going to charge me extra for waiting on your indecisive ass."

Alex and I are going to a Spanish club in the next town over tonight. She's sitting beside me, scrolling through her mass amounts of texts from men. None of which she plans on securing a relationship with. I have always admired that about her. Since she became my closest friend nearly eight years ago she's been able to go through so many flings without ever attaching feelings to them. I sit beside her, deciding whether I should feel envious of that trait or not.

Alex is beautiful. She's always perfectly kept and every man she talks to makes a point of noticing. She's wearing her signature black dress that slits in the back and cuts straight across her chest. Her hair is a few shades darker than mine and runs all the way down her back. Her curls always stay in perfect contact, even when she wakes up the next morning after an eventful night out. Though she's known for her looks and her killer personality, she's also known for controlling every situation. No man ever does anything she doesn't want him to. She's got balls. That's why she's my best friend.

I am an extrovert, but beside her personality you can hardly see me. Guys like to hang out with us at clubs because we look like sisters; twins almost. We have the same body shape, dark chocolate eyes, and even darker brown hair. Her hair is always a bit longer, her body is a bit thinner, and her eyes have an extra sparkle. I don't mind this. I like lurking in the shadows sometimes. I'm just pickier than she is. I think most guys know it and it scares them.

"Jos?" she questions. I look at her half buzzed and attentive. "Let's just make this night about us. I'm honestly a bit sick of guys. We've seen enough, we know what they're about and I've had enough sex for a lifetime."

We're both only twenty-two, but I agree. She pulls a small bottle of vodka out of her purse and swigs it back, passing it to me when she decides she's had enough. I take it and nurse it during the next twenty minutes until we get to the club. When we arrive, we trip out of the taxi and onto the cement. My ankles twist over top one another, causing my heels to make a loud clack. As I catch myself, I head towards the entrance of the bar. Dim lights cascade over dancing teens trailing all the way out to the patio. I've never been here before, yet I can already feel a sense of familiarity fading through me. We receive a stamp from the bouncer and proceed in through the entrance of the building.

"Do you see how many guys are here?" Alex almost shouts as she nudges my shoulder.

I don't notice until I look up from trying to concentrate on not tripping in these shoes. She's right; the ratio of men to women is about 60:40. Tonight is going to be a good one.

Though only two hours earlier Alex and I made a pact to give up men forever, she's completely forgotten it, and so have I. I'm not thinking of myself in this moment though. I'm fixated on being an impeccable wing-woman to Alex. We pick a seat up at the bar and choose our typical poison: vodka cranberry. We stir our straws slowly, contemplating how we're going to win over the men sitting directly across from us. It doesn't seem like this will be much of a challenge because one of them is already heading towards us. Alex parts from her stool to open up space for the person approaching us and his friend. She lunges to my side and intertwines her fingers with mine, insinuating that we are a package deal. The guy on the left who has just introduced himself as Dan has caught Alex's attention. I can tell by the way she's twirling a strand of her hair around in her fingers as she speaks. Dan isn't my type and I don't think he's Alex's either. I think she's just challenging herself to capture his attention. It's working.

To Dan's right is Charlie, who stands a whole foot shorter than me. He has light blond hair, flushed cheeks, and absolutely nothing to say. The three of us, excluding Charlie, go back and forth with typical bar banter. The simple things, like where we work, where we went to school and what we do as a pastime. I notice my buzz is wearing down because everything is becoming clearer. This is either due to a lack of alcohol or Charlie draining the life out of me. My mind drifts back to when I stumbled out of the taxi. How did I go from that, to this? There's nothing that I hate more than being completely sober in a room full of drunk people.

Alex nudges my shoulder and tells me that Dan bought a bucket of beers and they're going back outside on the patio to "get to know each other". She's brought my attention back to a conversation that I wasn't missing.

She says this while grabbing one of the opened bottles and taking a swig. Now I know that she's completely gone because she hates beer and she's just finished half the bottle in only a matter of sips.

I watch Alex and Dan fade into the doorway behind me and take that as my cue to escape Charlie for a few minutes.

"I'll be right back," I say, jumping down from my chair before he has the opportunity to oppose. Not that he would.

I make my way through the crowd of people dancing on each other. As I walk towards the staircase, I realize I'm not as sober as I thought. The buzz is coming back slightly. When I make it through to the other side, my hand grips a warm railing that trails all the way down a winding staircase and into the basement of the building. I walk into the bathroom and look up into the mirror. I see a girl who is overly touched up and unimpressed.

"What am I doing here?" I ask myself, looking into the mirror as if I'm expecting an answer.

I pull out my phone and type a message to Alex, "Charlie is a no-go." I see her start to type, and then the message goes away.

I make my way back upstairs. Retracing my steps hoping to reach the same barstools I was once sitting at. This place is fairly simple to navigate. One big square with a ton of people crammed into the middle. It's almost 1:00a.m. now and the room seems so much smaller. There are twice as many people who are twice as intoxicated as they were before I ventured downstairs. I squeeze my way through the sea of warm bodies and sweat. As I'm trying to manoeuvre my way out, a girl swings around while she's dancing, and her fist makes contact with my vodka cranberry. It spills all over my legs and shoes. I don't know why I'm still carrying it around.

"I am sssssooooo sorrryyyy," she says slurring her words loudly at me.

"It's alright," I reply.

I'm annoyed. Not annoyed enough to make a scene though. I'm one of the least confrontational people that I know. If it were Alex that had her drink spilled all over her new outfit, the situation would've taken a very drastic turn.

I wipe the red juice off of my legs and onto the floor. The girl starts patting at my legs with a napkin that she pulls out of the pocket of her skirt. I put my hand out to stop her.

"Honestly, don't worry about it," I say calmly.

I walk away from her while shaking my damp hands off. I see the empty seat where I was sitting and next to it is Charlie, right where I left him. I don't think that Alex has any intentions of leaving anytime soon so I think it's time I try making the most of this situation. I quickly walk back to the seat, draping my arm around Charlie. I swing around in front of him still holding onto the back of his neck. Maybe if I push him a bit he'll open up.

"So funny thing, some girl just spilled my drink all over me. Any chance you know where Alex is so I can get a new one?" just as the last word leaves my mouth, my jaw drops and my arm quickly removes itself from around his neck, shooting to my side. This is not Charlie. Charlie left at some point and sitting in front of me now is a stranger.

"Why did you move your hand? I liked it there," he says flatly. He has an arrogance about him that intrigues me.

"My friend was sitting here just a minute ago," my face is hot. He cuts me off to save the embarrassment.

"Yes, your friend Alex told me that you might need someone a little more interesting to talk to, so she called Charlie out to the patio and sent me in here."

I'm taken back by how well he remembers everyone's names. "Charlie and Dan are my friends from school," he continues, answering my unsaid question.

We sit quietly for a moment. For some reason it isn't awkward at all. Kind of like when you see an old friend for the first time in a while. His eyes are piercing. They are delicate and seductive. The more that I focus on them, the more I forget where I am. It's hard not to fall into a trance.

"So, you were saying someone spilled their drink on you?" he asks. The silence is broken.

"Yeah, it was that girl dancing over there," I gesture to the short blonde girl in the neon skirt and tube top.

"Here, we can share mine," he says sliding his glass towards me.

Normally I'd hesitate to accept this offer. I won't even share my drinks with Alex. Something inside me feels a strong desire to put my reservations aside. I press the cold beer to my lips and take a sip. This beer tastes a lot better than I remember.

Now that the shock of recent events has worn off, I take a second look at the stranger in front of me. I scan his face, looking at how intense his features are. He has jet-black hair that curls at its ends. It's pushed back and effortlessly hanging in place. His eyes are hazel and his brows accompany the shape of his face perfectly. The attraction I feel is startling me. I want to read him and see whether he likes what he sees too or if he's just trying to entertain his friends. He seems unbothered by this. I've never felt this comfortable with a stranger before, especially a stranger that I find this attractive. This could be a problem.

We begin to talk back and forth. I'm answering a series of questions about the kind of books I like to read and about how I met Alex. He's firing questions between sips as if it's a game to see how quickly he can get to know me. Not once talking about himself; I don't mind this. I'm used to every conversation with a guy being one-sided on their end.

"Have you been here before?" I ask. Realizing that there are far more important questions I could be asking him. Like what his name is.

"No, it's my first time here. I was actually ordering a cab to get out of here before we started talking. I hate places like this," he answers.

I nod in agreement. "It's my first time here too," I say.

"I don't really like coming out to clubs anymore," he states.

"Why's that?" I ask, cutting him off eagerly.

"Ever since about a year ago I haven't been able to-" he stops. Almost as if he's holding himself back from exposing his vulnerability to me too soon.

"Anyway, it's not important…" he trails off. "Dan and I are heading back to my house with a few people once my cab gets here if you want to come."

I open my mouth to speak, but he interrupts. "And Alex already told me she's in."

He doesn't even wait for my response, looking down at his phone to see that his ride is here. He stands up and says, "OK, he's here. Let's go get everyone."

I follow him blindly outside. It's pitch black besides the hanging lights that we saw on the way in. I pull out my phone and realize that it's now 2:30a.m. and I've been talking to this guy for almost two hours. I still don't know his name.

The van pulls up and it's a seven-seater. Alex and Dan shuffle into the far back seats, followed by Charlie and two girls who claim the middle row. One of them is the little blonde girl who spilled her drink on me. Now the only seat left is the passenger seat. I don't think this is going to work. I'm looking for someone to state the fact that there isn't enough room for all of us when my nameless new friend leans through the passenger window and starts a conversation with the driver. I see him shake hands with the man as if they know each other and he continues to open the door.

He steps back to face me, reaching his hand out to shake mine.

"I'm Fallon by the way," he says with a smile.

Chapter Two

"I'm Josephine, it's nice to meet you," I say taking his hand to shake it.

He opens the door and sits in the seat. He grabs my wrist and pulls me to sit on his lap. I think to myself "this cannot be legal". He then plugs his phone into the driver's van to play music. A mix of old 90's songs blast throughout the van, the kind that everyone knows the words to. Our singing begins to echo and I look to the very back seat to sing along with Alex. The windows are open, and everyone's hearts are light. We let the breeze carry us over the roads, not caring how loud we're being. It's like we have known these people forever.

After twenty minutes of driving and one stop at McDonald's, we pull up to the gate of a house along the lakeshore. The driver rolls down his window and types in a code, allowing for the thick gates to slowly open in front of us. As we drive through, we see a beautiful grey and black house that cascades well over the trees in the lot. The driveway stretches on for what seems like miles. It's dark, but I can see flowers and plants neatly lining the sides all the way up to the four-car driveway. When the car meets the front of the house, it stops. Everyone has their faces pressed to the window in awe. The house is lit up with bright pot-lights and glass hugs every corner. It's just dark enough to hide what's inside. It looks brand new. This can't be Fallon's house.

Just as quickly as the thought enters my head, Fallon moves his hand from off my knee and opens the garage door with a button on his key chain. I feel my eyes widen.

"Is this your house?" I blurt out.

"Yup," he says guiding me off him and out of the van.

I faintly hear everyone in the car talking back and forth. I hear Dan let out an, "I told you," followed by a giggle from Alex.

We all cram outside as fast as we can. I see Fallon slide an extra twenty dollars to the driver and he begins to walk into the garage.

"Well, come on," he says, raising an eyebrow and letting a small half-smile cross his face. We all follow behind him.

While waiting for him to turn the key to the door, I notice how tall he is. This is only my second time standing next to him. He's well over six feet tall. Just as he reaches for the door, I see the fabric of his white shirt line the muscles on his back. I try to stop myself from staring too long.

We enter through a hallway on the side of his house and follow him to the front door where the room opens up. My mind is racing. This is probably the nicest house I've ever seen, and he's only twenty-five. Dan and Charlie have already taken their shoes off and have thrown them into the hallway. They are clearly very comfortable here.

Fallon switches on a light, slowly illuminating an entire floor of a perfectly set up home. It looks completely untouched. I slowly take off my shoes and hold them in my hands. Fallon turns to me and grabs them, opening his closet and neatly placing them along with the rest of the shoes. He places his hand on the arch of my back and walks us all into his living room. I sit next to Alex and she shoots me a wide-eyed look as if she's wordlessly asking me what this place is. She turns back around to face Dan with her legs slung over his lap. They chat back and forth with one another; they both seem to be happy.

I think I'm in such shock because I'm comparing my lifestyle to Fallon's and it doesn't match up at all. I live in a one-bedroom apartment downtown. My place has old curtains, my mattress lies on the floor without a bed frame, and dishes pile up in the sink, with no desire to be washed or put away. We are extremely different. Fallon has his life put together and I don't. For some reason though, I'm drawn to him.

When I look over at him mixing away at an array of drinks in his kitchen, I become stuck on his face. His hands and body are moving happily to the rhythm of the music playing in the background of his home. However, the expression on his face doesn't match. He looks dreadfully handsome and horribly sad all at the same time.

His exterior and personality match this house so well. Anyone who met him for even a second would understand this. The lights hanging underneath his kitchen cupboards leave a blissful glow that reflects off the marble countertops. He's busy grabbing different bottles in his liquor cabinet to fill crystal glasses, topping them with ice and mixing them by hand. I walk up and lean over the counter across from him.

"Those look really good," I say flicking my eyes from the glasses and up to him. "Are you expecting a lot of people?" There are nearly thirty full cups sitting between us.

"I think Dan invited some of our friends from class. He's here all the time so I kind of let him do whatever he wants," he answers. Just as he lets the words out, we hear a loud bang on the door.

Fallon smiles and calls out, "they're here, Dan."

Charlie and Dan get up off the couch and open the door letting a flood of people in. Handshakes and warm welcomes are given and before I know it, the music is ten times louder. People are grabbing drinks and spreading throughout the room. They dance and talk loudly. His home now resembles a much nicer version of the club.

"Here, take one of these over to Alex, I think you girls will like it," Fallon says before turning to walk down the hallway.

I take the green drink over to my friend. She grabs it and gives it a try.

"This is so damn good," she confirms, chugging it down. When she's finished, she places the empty glass on a table beside the couch.

"So," she starts. "I did well, didn't I?"

Already knowing the answer I shake my head, smiling.

"You're welcome," she says, mocking me.

Song after song passes, and we're having so much fun dancing with everyone. As I finish each drink, more and more appear on the counter. Alex and I perform all of our signature moves, both feeling the positive energy of this party. As I begin to spin around, my body stops in front of Fallon, who's opening his arms for me to dance with him. At the same time, Dan comes to sweep Alex away.

"How many of those have you had?" he questions.

"I'm not too sure," my voice is light and airy. Obviously more than he has. In fact, I haven't seen him with a single drink since we left the club.

Not much is said as we dance. Every word I want to say is passing through my eyes, to his. His eyes are so intense. Calming even. We dance naturally with each other, closely and almost intimately. There's something that I can see in him that I haven't felt in anyone else. It's more than just a simple spark. I can feel my face flush more with each movement. He finally pulls me closer to him, noticing how tired I am after who knows how long we've been doing this. Resting my head on his shoulder, we are now slow dancing in a room full of people who are not. Each time he looks down at me, I feel his stare. His soft cheeks brush against mine and I can feel the warmth of his mouth. I think of when we were back at the club, when he was exposing a side of himself to me that he didn't mean to. Here I am now, holding hands with him, our lips almost touching, but he's not letting himself get close enough for me to really see him. I drape my hands around his neck and his hands trail down my back, pulling me further in.

After only seconds I hear Alex's voice, "Josie, Josie!" She's yelling from across the room.

"You'd better go," Fallon suggests, "I have a few things I need to take care of anyway."

I nod, "Let's do this again, soon?"

He smiles in agreement. I walk over to Alex and Dan is nowhere to be seen.

"Come outside with me, I need a smoke," she says.

Alex only smokes when she's drunk. She won't admit to it, even when I show her photos of herself the next day. She says they're Photoshopped.

She takes my hand and we walk to the main entrance where the coats are all lined in Fallon's closet. They are neatly put away. It shows that he cares, even about people he doesn't really know. I see Alex bend down and start digging through a pile of purses that are bunched in the corner, ones that don't belong to her.

"What are you doing?" I whisper loudly.

"What?" she questions. "Nobody's going to notice if one smoke goes missing." I roll my eyes at her.

"Ok, hurry up. We just met these people and you're stealing from them," I say frantically.

"I wouldn't say that. By the looks of it, you seem to know Fallon pretty well," she fires back. "Hold on, let me just grab this lighter."

She pulls out a red lighter from someone else's bag and we head to the porch.

"This place is insane," she states. "Dan told me that the three of them are in school to become pilots. They're all in their final year. They don't think Charlie will make it through though."

"Seems like you two talked a lot more than Fallon and I did," I say with an undertone of jealousy in my voice.

"That still doesn't explain how he lives in this huge house. Where did Fallon get this kind of money?" she seems concerned for me. "Dan did mention that he's been through a lot. Like some crazy shit," she adds.

I try to dismiss the comment. There's no point in dwelling on something I know nothing about.

"Have you gotten Dan's number yet? He's pretty cute. Doesn't seem like your type, though," I say.

"He's not really, but I like talking to him. I haven't stopped smiling since he walked up to us at the club," she says tugging at the ends of her dress. It makes me happy. This seems like a huge moment for her. Her first real connection with a guy beyond just looks.

"How did we find the perfect guys?" she asks.

I am questioning whether Fallon's really perfect or not. He hasn't told me anything about himself. Yes, we have this connection and attraction, but that doesn't mean a lot to me; I don't know anything beyond his name. My morals are coming into play. I need to slow myself down before I fall too hard. I'm known for going in too deep, too quickly. Something seems different about him though. It's not making things easy for me.

"Did Dan say anything about the 'crazy shit' that happened to Fallon?" I ask. I remember the look on his face earlier in the kitchen. I'm curious.

"No, he didn't. I didn't press too much though," she answers.

As Alex finishes her cigarette, she tells me she's going to go find Dan. Before she goes, she tells me that Dan asked her to stay over for the night so that she doesn't have to call another cab. Fallon never gave me this option. I walk inside and begin searching for him.

I look around the living room and into the kitchen. He's nowhere to be found. I walk up to Charlie, who has both of the blonde girls under his arms.

"Have you seen Fallon?" I ask.

"Yeah, I think he went upstairs," he answers.

I get a horrible feeling in my stomach. A feeling that maybe he's with someone else. I'm starting to feel protective of myself. I begin to head up the staircase questioning whether I should go looking for him or not. I feel a little uncomfortable wandering around his house without permission, but I put my feelings aside and force my legs to move. I want to know. I need to.

I get to the top of the stairs, poking my head into each room I pass. I finally find the master bedroom. I slowly open the door to a perfectly made bed, dimmed lamps, and an open patio door. I walk to the far side of the room and see him standing there, alone. His arms are slumped over a balcony that overlooks the water. It's beautiful. He isn't looking at it though. His hands are pressed to his head, gripping his hair. It looks like he's crying. I don't really know what to do. I don't have time to figure it out either. He realizes I'm standing behind him and he turns around.

"Sorry Josephine, have I been up here long?" he asks looking down at his wrist to see the time. "Shit, it's four in the morning".

"Are you okay?" I ask with worry. His hand slides down over his face, covering his eyes as he lets out a cry. Something is horribly wrong. I walk over to him and wrap my arms around his body.

"Come sit," I suggest. I walk him over to the small L-shaped couch in the corner.

We sit for a moment before the silence is broken. He turns to me with sadness in his eyes. Whatever is happening in his heart, I begin to feel it too. And I don't even know him.

He holds my cheek in his hand, "Josie, I really like you, which scares me enough on its own, but I can't do this to you."

His words fall from his lips and hit me hard. Harder than they should. I get the feeling that he's just coming out of a serious relationship. I've had my fair share of heartache and can understand. It's respectable that he wouldn't want to lead someone on. It seems like it's impossible for him to let himself be happy and it's hard to watch. For his sake, I put aside my pride in this moment.

"That's ok," I say sadly.

We have only just met; he doesn't owe me anything. I smile faintly, trying not to show my hurt.

"Can I sit with you for a while before I go? " I ask.

A million questions run through my mind. Why did he even invite me here? What happened to him? My thoughts stop. Before he has time to answer he kisses me. Long and slow. It's the softest kiss I've ever felt. His hand brushes hair from my face and I feel him let out a breath. It feels like he's letting something go that he's been holding inside for longer than one night.

He can see that I'm cold. It's just started raining and all I'm wearing is this short dress. He leans back and takes his sweater off, handing it to me to put on. We lay back on the couch, my head finding home on his chest. A tear rolls down my cheek. This feels so perfect and it will likely never happen again.

When the sun begins to rise, I press myself up off of him. We must have fallen asleep for a few hours. I softly brush my fingers through his hair trying not to wake him up. I look at him sideways for a moment, trying to memorize his face before getting up and heading to the front of his house. I quickly walk through a room of empty bottles and sleeping people. I put on my shoes and stand out on the front porch. It's hot and humid; I can already feel that it's going to be a scorching summer day. I begin looking for cab numbers in this area when the same van that took us here pulls up in front of me.

"Can I drive you home, Miss Josephine?" the driver asks.

I nod, climbing slowly into the backseat of the van. I rest my head back, tears falling down my cheek. I wipe them, trying to make it stop.

The driver pulls out from Fallon's driveway and heads towards the highway. I still haven't told him where I live.

"Do you need my address?" I ask the driver.

"No that's ok, Mr. Adams sent it to me when he called me to come and get you," he answers. I wonder how Fallon even got my address in the first place.

"Are you his driver or something?" I question.

"Yes, I've known Fallon since he was little. When his parents passed last year, he asked me to stay on and work around the house," he says. "I'm Pete, by the way. I'm not sure if Mr. Adams told you my name."

I try to hide my shock. I don't think he was supposed to tell me that. My heart sinks into the back of my chest. This explains so much. I wish I knew him before this happened, he must have been so full of life.

"You know," Pete continues, "in all my years of working for the Adams' family, I have not once seen Fallon with a girl. He must really like you. Have you two been together for a while?"

I don't answer his question. Not because I'm trying to be rude, but because I'm tired and disappointed. I wish

Fallon would have asked me to stay. It's difficult to imagine what Fallon must be going through but the only thing my thoughts keep circling back to is why he just let me leave.

●

Chapter Three
2015

When my eyes peel open for the day, the first thing I see is an ocean of white sheets. I pull them off of me and peek my head out. I run my hands through tangled hair and turn my head towards the bathroom door, listening to the echo of my husband's movements. I feel the steam from his shower seep out under the door. It leaves a fog on the wood that lines our floors. I look at my closet, trying to pick out an outfit to counter the mood I am feeling today. Black pants, and maybe a deep red shirt.

Joey's a rich man: polished, intelligent, and conserved. Every morning I watch him lift himself out of our bed, his strong body in control of every step he takes. Just like

he controls everything: safely and comfortably. I watch
him lift the tap next to mine, wait for it to warm and
watch as he runs his hands under the water to wash his
face. Before Joey, I went to college to study business,
although I was never really interested in it. I knew what I
wanted to be. I wanted to be needed by someone else.
When I met Joey, I knew what he could offer me so I
finished up my degree and we moved in together. He
told me that he'd always wanted someone who could
take care of him and who would hold together his
personal life while he went out and made money.

I hear Joey stop the shower and walk to his closet. He
always wakes up earlier than I do. By the time I'm
forcing myself awake, he's usually already taken a shower
and laid out his outfit. That's the life of a doctor, I guess.

My thoughts are interrupted by the sound of his voice.

"Good morning, love," he says walking over to me. He
greets me by brushing the hair from my face and giving
my cheek a kiss.

"Good morning," I reply, letting out a yawn.

He unwraps his towel from his waist and steps into his boxers. He pulls dress pants over them, followed by a white button up, and a tie. His frame is rough, yet he is meticulously put together. Most people would find this attractive. Over the years, its effects have faded in my mind.

"Can you get this for me?" he asks, holding the two ends of his tie, not knowing what to do with them.

I get onto my knees and inch over to the corner of the bed to meet his body, taking the tie from his hands and re-wrapping it around his neck.

"You know, one day you're going to need to learn how to do this on your own. I can't always be here when you need me," I tease. I'm not sure if this is a playful statement or not. Maybe it's a subconscious thought.

"Don't say that," he says, letting a small frown line his lips. He wraps one arm around my waist, pulling me in for a hug before turning and trailing off through the doorframe. I follow behind him.

Joey sits at the kitchen table, pulling out his iPad and looking through the news app, his glasses pressed on his nose. A serious look captures his face. This is his reading look. I grab an elastic from my wrist and tie up my hair, pulling out the frying pan from under the sink and eggs from the fridge. The coffee machine automatically starts behind me, brewing his favourite bold cup. I grab it and place it in front of him. He takes his coffee black; he says milk and sugar contradict the purpose of the drink. I don't agree with that: I can't drink coffee without milk.

I fry up his eggs in avocado oil with a side of rye toast, no butter. People say Joey's a particular man. He works viscously hard and knows what he wants. I think that's what attracted me to him. He took a long time to understand. I still sometimes find myself doing things that he says aren't right. Not just any woman could be his wife. There are so many things he needs done in a day that I'm hardly ever home. I watch him eat, wiping his mouth after every bite. He tells me about the weather difference from here, in Toronto, to where he's going in Washington for a conference this coming weekend. I listen attentively, trying to soak up every word.

"Thank you for breakfast, excellent as per usual," he says, piling his dishes by the sink. "Can you make sure you don't forget the additions to today's list that I left on the counter? I thought of a few things I need done while I was in the shower." He points to the counter beside the fridge. I see a crisp, yellow paper lying neatly beside a straightened pen.

"Of course," I walk over to pick it up and put it in my purse.

Joey heads to the door, swinging back his last sip of coffee. He places his empty mug on the table beside the shoe rack, leaning down to tie his shoes. I wish him off and head upstairs to get ready for work.

It takes me about two hours to get ready every day. Today I begin by curling my hair to drop thoughtfully down my back and spray the top down. I continue to tuck it's ends behind my ears and brush it into a slick hold. I put on my plain black pants, accompanied by my red blouse. Next, I begin my makeup routine. I spread foundation across my face, I fill in my sporadic brows; touch a dark brown shadow on my eyelids; and blink mascara onto my lashes. I raise a fake smile to coat blush onto my cheeks and push a dark red lipstick onto my lips. After deciding I'm ready, I make my bed and pick up after Joey. I follow a trail of where he's been this morning which involves putting away hair gel, toothpaste, and his clothes from the night before. When I'm finished this, I head downstairs.

I never eat breakfast. I always start my day with a cold latte from a local coffee shop just down the street. I grab my keys off of the marble counter and head out the door. It's really sunny out, and the air is fresh and nips my cheeks as I unlock my car. It is only 9:00a.m. and I'm on the clock. I'm running a few minutes behind schedule, making me late for my shift as housewife.

I have more than usual on my schedule today because this weekend I'm going out of town to visit my good friend, Alex. I've wanted to go to Alex's place for such a long time. Her and Dan have recently gotten engaged and are having a party to celebrate. Though Alex and I talk every day, just like we did when we were kids, I haven't seen Dan since Joey and I got married three years ago. It's the perfect time for me to go visit Alex.

It's about a three-hour drive to her place past Muskoka. She's there alone most of the time because Dan's a pilot. He has two weeks on, one week off schedule. Her and I live pretty similar lives. Although she works a few hours a week at a publication downtown, she comes to see me all the time. Once I'm done getting groceries, taking Joey's suits to get pressed, selecting furniture for our summer house, and finding someone to come fix one of the bathrooms on our main floor, I'll meet with Alex outside of her office.

I start the engine of my car and head across town to the bakery where Joey likes his groceries from. I sample cheeses and vinegars as I fill my basket with fresh bread and other pre-made casseroles. I make sure I'm being diligent and paying attention to my watch. As I check out, I put the address of my next location on my phone. I load the groceries into my car and head off out of one parking lot and into another. I weave quickly in and out of stores, trying to speed through my tasks; I'm anxious to see Alex. I haven't talked to her since the engagement. I only know what she told me over the phone, and that was an inconsistent story, interrupted by a lot of screams and laughs.

I park my car just outside of her office. The restaurant is beside her building and it's one of the most popular in town. When I begin to walk over I can see that Alex is waiting for me on the patio. She stands up to give me a huge hug and says she missed me.

"Show me the rock," I say grabbing her left hand and twisting the diamond from the back of her small finger to the front. "It might be a bit too big," I say softly, trying not to bring her mood down.

"Oh, I know," she says laughing. "Dan's already ordered the right size. I wanted to keep this one on so I can show it off." Very typical for Alex.

"So, how did it happen? tell me everything!" I say with excitement.

She goes on to tell me that Dan took her to a lilac field an hour south of where I live and had the owners pluck out the words "marry me" in flowers. He had candles and blankets waiting there for them to watch the stars at night afterwards. Very typical for Dan.

She then dives into a long rant about her plans, the dates and what she needs to do. I'm not surprised that they're getting married. I think back to the night they met at that bar and how happy she was. He changed her life forever. Mine too. He took the responsibility from me of taking care of her and showed her how to care for herself. I will always love Dan for that.

"Josie, will you be my maid of honour?" she asks abruptly. Tears begin to coat her cheeks. I can tell she's nervous.

"You didn't even need to ask," I say smiling. "Anything you need, I've got it."

We start talking about the party this weekend. I've now been given the task of ordering all of the food and decorations to her house to be set up by Dan and his friends. I don't mind this: party planning has always been a passion of mine. Business school was my parent's idea.

"I wanted to talk to you about something else, not just my engagement," Alex says softly. I feel a bit of panic in my chest when she says that.

"Is something wrong?" I ask.

"No. Well, I don't think so. It's just," she pauses. "Do you remember Fallon?"

The name hits hard like a big brick of memories. I hold my face straight. I haven't heard his name in ages.

"Yes," I say slowly.

"He's going to be Dan's best man," she says. "I was worried if I told you, you wouldn't want to be so involved in the wedding."

I hadn't really considered this possibility. He's just a guy that I met at a party once and I'm a bit irritated that she thinks so little of me. I'm married now and she knows that. Thoughts fly through my head, thinking of something to say, until I remember flashes of the months after I met him. I was a mess. Embarrassingly enough, I didn't go out for weeks after he told me he couldn't see me. And he didn't see me after that night. My life consisted of long nights eating ice cream, drinking wine in my apartment, and looking like a mess. That's until I met Joey. I haven't thought of Fallon much since then.

"I know why you'd think that, but Alex, that was five years ago," I say trying to cover my shock.

"You were just so hurt," she says looking down, swinging the huge ring on her hand rapidly around her finger. She looks back up at me, "The good thing is you probably won't have to see him until the wedding. He's not coming to our engagement party."

"I think I can handle that," I say with a deep feeling of disappointment. I narrow this feeling down to the hurt of rejection.

We begin to talk about all that needs to happen in the next three days before her party. We decide that she should do "masks and mimosas" for her theme. Everyone will be dressed elegantly with a mask to paint the illusion of mystery. She loves this idea. She says it reminds her of Fifty Shades of Grey. Of course, this is her favourite book. And the only one she has ever read.

"Ok, so I'll have all of the supplies, food, and champagne ordered and sent to your house. Just make sure Dan's there the day of so he can set up. I have to work until

4:00p.m. that day and it will take me a few hours to get there," I explain.

"God Jos, you're so organized," she says with relief. "I'm so lucky to have you." She hugs me as we part ways.

When I get home that night, Joey's not there. I unpack all of the swatches and the furniture he asked me to pick up for him from my trunk. I pull out my phone to see a text.

"Hey hon, I've been scheduled into an emergency surgery. I'm not sure when I'll be home. Love you," he writes.

I let out a sigh as most of our nights are like this. I start the casserole that I bought at the bakery for Joey, along with a handful of sweet potato and asparagus. For myself, I make two pieces of toast and open a bottle of wine. I let his food cook in the background until it's finished, then I take the tray out from the oven and plate the food. I shut everything down in the kitchen before I pull out my laptop and fire away at emails for Alex's party until my eyes fade shut and I am out for the night.

--

The next morning, I wake up to the crash of my laptop hitting the floor. I pick it up and pull the blanket off of my knees. My alarm starts buzzing frantically and I pick up my phone to shut it off. It is 7:00a.m. and I'm just in time to see Joey off for the day. I wander up the stairs and into our room. Our bed is still made and it looks untouched. When I come back downstairs, I see that the food I made him is untouched as well. I slide it into the compost bin and toss the dish in the sink. I pull my phone out to read another text from Joey, "it's going to be an all-nighter. I should be home by the time you're off for the day."

I wipe off my makeup, change my clothes, and am off to another day of running around for him.

The first task on my list of stops is to find an outfit for the party on Friday. I find a black and silver mask with a long feather tracing up its side. I'm not sure what I'm going to wear yet, but I'll make it work. In the next store I find and buy a pair of shoes that match it: tall black heels with a diamond studded strap to go around the ankle. It seems stupid to base an outfit on a mask and shoes, but that's just how I shop. After three or four stores I find a beautiful deep pink dress. It almost shows as a bright red. It has thick straps that flow to a sweetheart neck in the middle. The cleavage is covered with mesh. It's perfect, and it fits beautifully. I take a picture of myself in it and send it off to Alex for her approval. She sends me back a photo of herself pretending to be shocked, with a caption that reads, "that's the one!"

I pay for it at the front of the store and head home to put everything away. When I get home, I open my email to see an array of instructions for the party. I fulfil the requests and send my credit card information along with my own list of instructions. I then put together a document full of times that Dan needs to be available to get everything ready.

--

It's now Thursday evening and I'm laying out my clothes for tomorrow. Joey's home and he's starting to pack his bag for his weekend away.

"What do you think I should bring?" he asks grabbing an empty bag from his closet.

"Check the closet one more time," I answer.

He walks into the closet and flicks on the lights, pulling out a bag packed with everything he could possibly need on his trip. Joey has done this so many times by now, I can put together a travel bag for him in less than ten minutes.

"You're an angel," he says, sweeping me up into a hug. The past few days he's been in such an amazing mood. I'm scared to break it because Joey can be so hot and cold. One minute he's expressing his love for me and the next he explodes in anger. This is a side I've only seen a handful of times over the years, but with the stress of his job, he's been losing control more frequently.

He stands beside me and whispers into my ear, "Now, you better be good while I'm gone."

The way he says this sends a chill through me.

"I will," I say, quickly kissing him to ease his tension.

"Now let's see how good you really are," he walks over to the bag and rummages through it. "Josephine," he says sternly. "You do realize that you've forgotten my passport in here, right?"

He begins to walk back over to me. I freeze up. I can't keep messing up like this.

"You could've messed up my whole trip. If I got there and needed to come back to get that, I would've lost it!" he yells, as if he is not on the brink of losing it right now.

He takes me by the shoulders and pushes me onto the bed. He lies on top of my still body, pinning my arms up over my head with one of his hands and squeezes my cheeks harder than he should with the other. I let out a gasp because his grip is so tight that it's hurting.

"I'm sorry," I say quietly.

"You should be," he replies, releasing me. "Now, I have to go, and you made me make our last few minutes together terrible. I'll see you soon, I love you."

The words hit me like a hard slap. I don't know how he can say he loves me and do something like this all in the same breath.

When I'm certain he's left the house I jump into my bed and pull the covers over me. I let the pressure of the heavy blanket on top of me, comfort me. I let out a cry that breaks into sobbing and I continue to cry all night.

--

There isn't a moment where I think that things between Joey and I are unfixable or that I think about leaving. I want to wait under the blankets for him to come back, but I have to get up now because it's the morning of Alex's party.

I do my makeup early so that when I am done my tasks I can come home, get dressed, and leave. As I do my makeup, I feel a pain in my wrists. There are faint bruises from where Joey grabbed me last night. I cover them up with foundation, patting them with powder to give them a realistic finish. No matter how much I apply, it doesn't seem to work. If I can see through it, so will everyone else. I realize that I'm running behind, so it will have to do.

Today's chores are to put together Joey's 30th birthday party. It's supposed to be a surprise party however, he's asked me to put it together so it's not much of a surprise. I'm supposed to call his closest friends and coordinate what they should get for him based on a list I've conjured up. I also have to put together decor, food, and order a cake. I must do all of this as well as prepare for the arrival of his new car. He wants me to expand our garage so he can fit the car I've ordered inside of it, plus the cars he currently drives.

Joey has been collecting cars a for lot longer than I've known him. He has a Lamborghini, a Ferrari, and a Mustang. He bought the Mustang himself and the other two cars were gifts from his father. He told me that this year he wants something more practical that he can drive to work.

I phone some contractors to come take a look at the house on Monday and see if they can have it ready in four months for Joey's party. When I'm done this, I have to get Joey an outfit to go with his party theme, "Casino Night," which again, he picked himself. He wants me to re-decorate our entire four-floored home into a casino, equipped with blackjack tables, slot machines, and entertainment. I'm sure I can do it; I've thrown huge parties for him before. I'm just not in the mood to do it today.

It's now 4:00p.m. and I've already met with the contractors and browsed all of Party City. My car is full of decorations that Joey probably won't approve of. I need to go home and get ready because I don't have much time. I walk into my room and slip on my dress. I pair it with long diamond earrings and a bracelet Joey bought for me on our wedding day. I slip the bracelet over my wrist, adjust my hair and re-touch my lipstick. I grab my feathered mask from off of my dresser and throw it into my purse. I'm ready to go.

I drive as fast as I can down the highway so that I'm not late, but I still end up coming to a halt in Toronto's traffic. I send a text to Alex saying that I might be late and that I'll be there by the time dinner is served. After a few hours of driving, I pull into her driveway and walk up the lot to her front door. My mind has been running so quickly since last night. This evening will be a nice distraction from it.

I walk into Alex and Dan's party holding two gifts for them. A blender that Joey insisted I buy Dan, along with a gold-chain necklace that I picked out for Alex, long before she was engaged. Joey thinks he knows Dan so well, when realistically he's only met him twice. He sees Dan's posts on Facebook about cooking and his new kitchen renovation, and suddenly he thinks this blender is something Dan needs. I mean, I'm sure anyone would like a thousand-dollar blender, but Alex and Dan have a cook - they don't need it.

Tonight, their house is completely swamped with people. It's overly secluded without a neighbour for miles and cottage-like while somehow remaining modern; just like them. Dan gives me a hand with the gifts when he sees I'm struggling to carry them both. Once he puts the boxes down, he brings me in for a hug. His eyes are light, and his voice is soft; he hasn't changed a bit. Seeing him makes me sad that we can't see each other often anymore. He has the same bizarre work schedule as Joey. Well, that's the excuse that Alex and Dan give me.

"How have you been, it's so nice to see you, Josie," he says, pulling apart from our hug.

"It's good to see you too, it's been so long. Congratulations by the way," I say, nudging him playfully, "I heard the proposal was so romantic. You did good my friend."

"Thank you, it's about time I locked things down with Alex. I needed to catch up to you and Joey. How is he? I haven't seen that guy since right after you two got married," he says, trying not to draw on the reasoning behind it.

"He's doing well," I try and think of something to distract from the fact that he lost his mind again last night. "He's away this weekend at a meeting. He's just been hired on at a hospital in the States. In Washington, actually. He told me to tell you that he's really happy for you," I ramble.

"That's amazing," he says. "You made it just in time by the way. There should be a name card for you close to where Alex and I are sitting at the end of the table. Go take a seat, and I'll have a server bring you some chardonnay." He still knows me so well.

I walk through a crowd of people to the longest table I have ever seen. It looks like it seats about forty. I don't know how this table fits in their house. I find my name tag, "Josephine Parker" and take a seat, pulling a dark blue napkin over my knees. A server reaches over my shoulder and places my drink in front of me. I let out a "thank you," as she walks away. I hear a glass being tapped and everyone looks to the left of the table to where Alex is beginning to make a speech. I reach in front of me to grab my glass and as I take hold of it, I look up to meet the hazel eyes of Fallon.

Chapter Four

We're all wearing masks, but I know it's him. I quickly look over at Alex, trying to think of something to say to Fallon once she's finished with her toast. I don't think he'll let me ignore him. Although, he has done a really good job ignoring me over the past five years.

"I just wanted to quickly say thank you to everyone who made it here today. I know you all can hardly believe that I found someone to put up with me," she says. Everyone lets out a laugh. "It's been a long road and we're so excited to finally be at this point. These past few years have been the best of my life," she pauses to take a breath. "And I'm thankful for every day I have with Dan.

I just wanted to say a special thank you as well to my maid of honour, Josie, and to Dan's best man, Fallon, for helping us plan the party tonight," she lifts her glass in the air and suddenly I feel like Fallon being here is not a coincidence. Alex knew Fallon was going to show up and she lied to me about it anyways. "I won't keep you waiting to eat any longer, I know you all must be starving," she says as she sits down.

The servers start bringing out the food all around us. I see Fallon raise his glass, looking for me to cheers with him, and I do. He puts his glass down and lifts his mask to uncover his face. His features are just as breathtaking as they were the last time that I saw them, making it even harder to comprehend the situation.

"Josephine, it's nice to see you," he says deeply. He says my name too easily.

"It's good to see you too, Fallon," I reply.

I cut straight to the point, not caring that there are thirty-eight other people sitting at the table. They all seem too busy talking anyways, with no time to listen to my relationship issues.

"Alex told me that you weren't going to be here tonight," I say sharply.

"Is that going to be a problem?" he lets out a smile. The same stupid grin that made me dance with him in front of everyone the first night we met.

"No," I reply. "I just-"

He cuts me off, "I know," he says, completely breaking his character, "it was hard for me to see you too. They told me that you wouldn't be here either." And now Alex and Dan's ploy to get us in a room together makes sense.

I knew that Alex and Dan have never approved of Joey. They see the way he treats me and they don't like it. Ever since we got back from our honeymoon, they saw Joey slowly become more and more demanding. Before my wedding Alex had been holding in a lot of her feelings about Joey. She didn't want to put pressure on me with all of the wedding stress so when Joey and I came home from our trip, she laid it all out on the table. I'm not surprised that they dislike Joey, but I didn't think they would put Fallon and I in the same room, at the same table, and basically force us to talk.

"Don't worry, just enjoy your dinner and we can talk later. I have some explaining to do," Fallon says. My head is rattling with adrenaline, this is too much all at once.

"OK..." I let out. As I finish speaking, a short girl with curt blonde hair slumps down beside him and intertwines her arm with his. She seems a little drunk, a bit like the girl from the bar the night Fallon and I met. I can't keep my eyes from rolling back. Our conversation comes to a crashing halt as soon as she sits. It's like he doesn't want me talking to this girl. She looks like she's maybe twenty-one, twenty-two. He turns his attention to her, the shift causing anger to rise within me. I remind myself that I didn't know Fallon at all, so I shouldn't be letting myself get upset by this.

I start talking to an old college friend, Maria who's sitting to my left. She tells me all about the travelling she's done since school ended. Last year she went backpacking through Europe; the year before she signed up to work at a resort in Mexico as a theatre performer; and before that she went on one of those year-long cruises with her girlfriend. I've already seen most of these events plastered on her social media. And I care much less for them the second time around.

The resentment I have for Joey grows stronger as I sit here talking with Maria. She's doing all of the things he'll never let me do.

"So, what have you been up to?" she questions. I rack my brain. *What have I been up to?*

I rest my hand on my chin, "you know what, I've just been so busy with work and helping Joey out with arranging his parties, there isn't much time for travelling. We've been planning a trip for next fall, though."

"Oh, that's great! You finally put the party planning business into play I see. I remember when we used to sit in our economics class with Alex and you'd draw setups for future clients. I'm so proud of you," Maria says, her words sting.

She wouldn't be so proud if she knew what I actually did for a living, and neither would Alex. She's my best friend and I still haven't admitted to her that I'm not a personal shopper anymore. I quit my job as soon as I moved in with Joey. I look over my shoulder to see Fallon and I think he might be listening, so I lie. "Yes, it's going really well," I say a little too loudly.

A pang of guilt shoots through me. I can now feel Fallon's stare as he drifts from the conversation with his blonde, twenty-year-old girlfriend, to mine. I can tell that he knows I'm lying. I cut a piece of chicken on my plate and fill my mouth, hoping that Maria takes this as a sign to keep eating. I look up quickly to see Fallon shaking his head and then turning to eat his food. I'm surprised that he's the one judging me. After all these years, it's almost like he's forgot how big of a liar he is. I scoff and sip my wine, listening to Maria continue on about her new girlfriend who she met while vacationing in Mexico. Her name's Clara. I picture how exciting Maria's life must be. She's one of the most outgoing people I know; a full-time optimist. To do what you want, when you want, must be nice. I often think that my life would have been like that if I hadn't met Joey.

--

An hour passes and almost everyone has finished desert: a really nice chocolate mousse filled into miniature cups.

The cups of mousse are sitting on top of plates and piled with raspberries. The berries trickle down the sides and onto the plates below. This desert is Alex's favourite. I shoot her a look, a wordless one, to show her how proud I am that she's getting married. I lift a spoonful of the mousse and give her a cheers in the air. She laughs, resting her head on Dan's shoulder and looking up at him with love in her eyes. I remember times when I thought I was in love. It's a hard reality to face knowing that feeling is not alive in my relationship with Joey anymore. I still care so deeply for him, but the feelings of passion between us left long ago. His passion has been replaced with anger, and mine, with pain. The repetitive motion of being his wife has grown tiring.

When I was younger it was all I wanted. I didn't know him back then like I do now. If I had, I'm not sure I would want this life for myself. He used to rush home every night, a hand full of flowers in his hand and dinner on the way from one of our favourite restaurants. I guess as time treaded on his love was left somewhere in the distance, waiting to be picked up by someone else. I just didn't feel the shift. Our weeks now start with laughter and long conversations on a Monday and by Friday he has forced himself back into the same miserable mould.

The tension is brutal sometimes. I try my best to do as he asks but it just never seems to be enough.

When I look up from my daze everyone has gotten up and gone into the other room. Everything is gone except me and a half a plate of food. I look down at my wrist and see that the black from my bruise is becoming more prominent. The foundation must have rubbed off on the fabric of my dress. I jangle my bracelet to try and cover it but it's too thin.

I sit back in shock over how the day is turning out. What could Fallon possibly need to talk about? A thousand scenarios fill my mind. I stand up and walk towards the chatter creeping around the corner. There are crowds of people dancing and talking. This is a party for adults, but it doesn't feel that way. Everyone I used to know is here, they're all just older; the same people in stretched out skin, wearing more conservative clothes, and with deeper voices. Half of them are parents now, which is why I'm surprised they have this kind of energy anymore. They all seem entirely different, yet the same. I pour myself a drink from the punch bowl and the berries inside dance around as the liquid pours down into the nozzle. The smallest things seem to amaze me these days. I'm a simple person, always finding myself trapped in irregular circumstances. I drop my arm down to my side and I feel the clasp on my bracelet begin to open from hitting off of the table. I step back to quickly and adjust it as Alex appears in front of me. I look up from my wrist and shake my head at her softly.

"What the hell, Al? You said Fallon wouldn't be here," I laugh.

"I know," she replies turning her head away from me. "He just hasn't stopped talking about you for five years. It's been a lot," she pleads. "He would never reach out on his own, I don't know why. He always just narrowed it down to thinking you were happy. We all know you're not." A silence follows. I can't be mad at her; it's her engagement party. I just don't know what to say to her.

"Okay..." I stare at her blankly. "How does this change the fact that I'm married?"

She doesn't really have an answer. She tells me that over the years Fallon has been asking her more and more about my life and that she hasn't given him any hints or insight. He clearly just wants to see into my world.

"He's wanted to talk to you ever since you married Joey," she says sadly.

"Okay, then why show up with some young blonde chick?" I ask.

"I honestly had no idea he was going to bring her. Dan was surprised too. He says he hasn't met any of Fallon's girlfriends since the night you guys went out. Fallon's a oddly private person and he has his secrets too…" she trails off.

"How's any of this my problem?" I snap.

"It's not," Alex says.

"Okay, great!" I lift my glass to her and walk outside. She follows me and we sit on plastic chairs lining the patio of her home. We're both quiet for a while and I can tell she feels bad. I'm just confused. I'm sorting out feelings that I've kept buried inside for this exact reason.

"You're right, Al," I start. "You know me and I'm not happy. But I've built my whole life around Joey and I can't just leave, he needs me. I know if I give him time, he'll come around. He really likes you guys, and neither of you ever gave him a chance," my eyes are watering.

She puts her hand on mine as I finish speaking. I don't even know why I'm defending him. My words always seem to betray my thoughts. Dan walks up behind us and places his hand on Alex's shoulder.

"Hey, baby," he kisses her head. He's had a few drinks by now and probably some shots too. It's his party, I don't blame him. He deserves all the happiness and I'm disappointed that they made this night about Fallon and I.

He slings his arm around Alex. "One hell of a party," he says winking at me.

"Don't sweat it," I answer.

"Are you coming to the bar? It closes soon and some of us are gonna take an Uber there across town," he says, tilting his head as he waits for an answer.

"No, you guys go, I'll stick around and clean up; you know I don't really do bars anymore…" I trail off, knowing I'm referencing the night we all last went to the bar and Joey got into a fight with Dan.

"You're the fuckin' best," he says before turning to leave. Alex and I both laugh at this as we watch Dan walk to the front door and shout, "Anyone coming to the bar, there are six Ubers on their way. Let's go!"

"Okay, my cue. I need to go take care of him," Alex says as she leans in to hug me. Her loose brown curls drape over my shoulder and a huge wave of her perfume falls over me. The same one she's always worn. She's one of the only consistencies I've had throughout the years. "Thank you so much," she pulls away and goes to get her shoes.

Once she's down by the driveway the sound of the darkness is left behind. Not that there's a physical sound for it, but rather a feeling of nothingness left by the conversation we just had. Alex and Dan light up the room everywhere they go, and their absence doesn't go unnoticed. I decide to wander inside, and I begin picking up bottles and masks. One, two, three, four... the counting becomes endless. The party is still alive, even though half of the crowd has left. Including, it seems,

Fallon and his girlfriend. When I'm done, I pour myself a huge glass of rum punch from the punch bowl, tilting the nozzle and watching the light pink liquid swirl around the glass, just as I did the first time. Nobody is drinking it, and I feel sober. I knock back glass after glass until it's empty and I finally feel a buzz. I put down my glass and walk into the kitchen, rummaging through the cupboards until I find another bottle of chardonnay.

"Fuck it," I say, and I pop the top to nurse the full bottle as if it were a single drink. Everyone who's still here is drunk, nobody will care. I lean back into the closed cupboard behind me and watch Alex and Dan through the glass of the front door. They're taking one more shot with Maria and Clara while waiting for their Uber's. One shot turns into two, two turns into three, and three turns into four. I watch each one of them drift further and further from being sober. I can feel the music pump louder through the walls and it feels like Alex's house has developed a heartbeat. I spin the now half empty bottle around, listening to its contents splash its edges and slide down into my mouth. I pull out my phone to see if Joey has texted me, but my eyes are met with a blank screen. The time reads 1:30a.m.

Dan's fist knocks the side of the front door, "the Uber's are here now, you sure you don't want to come?"

I nod, "it's okay. I'll stay behind and clean up a bit for you guys. I want to make sure everything's good here. It's the least I can do after everything you two have done for me."

I give him a quick wave, and he's gone again. I stand up, grabbing some more bottles off the table and put them into the sink. I take this as a perfect opportunity to call Joey and see if he made it to the conference safely. I walk out to the back patio and slide the door closed behind me. There's nobody out here, but me. I open my phone and its reflection shines brightly in the dark. I listen to the hum of nature and take a deep breath before hitting dial. It rings once and then the call stops. I try it again and get the same results. He must have turned off his phone. I put the phone back in my pocket and sit on the chair beside me tilting my head back and taking another sip. I'm now tipsy. I hear the door slide open and a voice speaks from beside me.

"Hey," it says.

I look over and see Fallon walking in front of me. He turns his back to the fence, propping himself up with his hands and resting his leg against the middle of it. He's wearing a dark grey sweater which completely contrasts the sharpness of his outfit. The hood's pulled up over his head, but the features of his face still remain prominent, almost seductive against the light. I try to remind myself that I'm mad at him.

I feel the music echo through the walls behind us. My mind wanders to the last time we were in this situation and my mouth follows.

"Funny meeting you here, again," I say, my words don't really make sense.

"Yes, it's been a while," he says looking down at his feet.

"Did you want some?" I tilt the bottle in his direction. He grabs it and sips.

"You didn't really leave me much," he says as he places its empty frame on the table beside me. A brief tension builds between us. I'm not sure if it's good or bad. My drunk mind tells me to break it.

"So, your girlfriend seems... nice," I start. I don't think I'm doing a good job at hiding my feelings.

"She's not my girlfriend," he replies sharply. "She's a friend." I think back to when they first arrived holding hands. I'm not sure friends do that.

"Not that it's any of my business, but I don't think she knows that," I say bluntly, which is unlike me.

Suddenly, he's like an open book. He's telling me about how he took her on a date earlier in the afternoon and she asked him to bring her to the party tonight. He felt like he couldn't say no. This type of dialogue with Fallon is foreign to me. I guess five years can change someone.

"Now she's gone to the bar with Alex and Dan," he says finishing his story.

"Bummer," I reply flatly.

This makes him laugh. It makes me laugh too.

"I've missed your laugh," he says, pulling his hand up to my face. "I saw it so many times that night it's been pressed into my brain."

He's staring intently. I go to remove his hand from my face and in one swift movement he takes hold of my wrist and examines my bracelet from Joey. I wince at his touch. He's pressing on my bruise. He then slides the bracelet down my arm and the faint light reflecting off of the doorway is shining right onto Joey's fingerprints.

"What the hell happened?" his eyes flash up to mine.

I try to muster up an explanation behind what it is, but Joey's fingerprints are so prominent it couldn't be anything else. It makes my face hot. I rip my hand away and he can tell by my facial expressions how it got there. I see him fill with anger.

"Josie, what the fuck?" he walks to the edge of the deck, visually upset, reacting like an angry husband would. "Can you stay with Alex? I'm sure she would let you. If not, you're staying with me. I don't care," he's speaking quickly. His eyes are wild, picking thoughts that scatter through his brain and throwing them at me. It's too much.

"Why do you even care?" I say, rolling my bracelet back into place. My first reaction is to defend Joey. Fallon seems hurt by my question but he knows what I mean by it. Mixed along the lines of a few simple words, I'm really saying that this wouldn't have happened if he didn't ask me to leave that night. And that reality leaves us both silent.

"I don't know what you want me to do. I'm married to Joey. I love him, Fallon. He's always given me everything I've needed. He stepped in when you left me to wonder what was so wrong with me," I say, my voice raising.

"You can't love him. How can you love someone who would do that to you?" he pauses. "Who knows what else he does. Alex and Dan have told me what an asshole that guy is."

"Think what you want but you obviously don't know the first thing about being in a relationship," I hate my words. Yet, I can't stop them from coming.

"You're right, I don't. I've never really had a meaningful one. If I could, it would have been with you," he says. His words confuse me. "We spent six hours together and those six hours have been the best of my life in the past five years. So yes, it's devastating to me that this is what your life turned out to be because of me."

"Fallon, stop," I cut him off. I'm drunk, but I still understand that nothing Joey's done is anyone's fault but mine.

I hadn't realized the severity of the events that took place in my life after I met Fallon. I gave the rest of myself to the first person who asked for it. I was just trying to cover up the hurt I felt. Joey and I got married so quickly and it only took a few months of us living together for him to start acting differently. We've never talked about the things that have happened between us; I haven't talked about them with anyone. The long nights of him screaming at me; all the times he's thrown things at me, grabbed me, even the times he's hit me. It doesn't happen very often, but he never addresses it and that worries me. It's almost like he doesn't realize what he's doing. Over time, I just stopped thinking about it and let it happen. It's as if his lack of realization started to rub off on me. Leaving me with no desire to stop him. Sometimes it's almost as if we both black out and whatever he does, we leave be. I've thought about leaving a few times; I've packed bags and left them in the closet so that when the time came to move them into my car it would be one swift movement, leaving the least amount of thought possible. A grab and go scenario. The only problem is that I would wait until the last minute and go through my bag, telling myself, "I don't really need this," and, "he'll notice if that's gone," until there's nothing left in the bag. Then I would put the bag back into its drawer and try again the next time.

My eyes are now watering, letting out fast streaks of tears. I go to wipe them and realize that my mask is still on. I lift it off of my face and put it down on the ledge. I place my elbows down beside his, looking out into the dark, trying to see what his eyes see. There's something calming about it. Standing beside him drives electricity through me, as if someone has lit an old spark and left it to burn, watching to see what it does. He puts his hand on top of mine, looping our fingers together. His hands are soft and warm, nothing like Joey's.

"It's gonna be okay, you know," he says softly.

"How can you be sure?" I ask, genuinely not knowing the answer.

"I can't," he replies. At least he's honest.

We're quiet for a minute. A full sixty seconds this time, I count. My mind is fading back to sobriety.

"You haven't changed much," I say turning to face him. "The only thing that's different is your hair," I pull at the curl falling down the side of his forehead. "Your eyes haven't changed either, " I pause. "And I can see you've still been working out," I say, trying to soften the thick depressing wall standing between us.

"I'd have to say the same about you. You look more mature though. Stronger, even. You look like you're more willing to be yourself. I like that," he says looking over at me.

"Well, I'm not a kid anymore," I reply.

"I know," he says, letting the smile fade from his mouth as he falls silent.

"Josephine," he says my full name. It echoes through me, reminding me of Joey so I quickly look away. After Fallon, my full name was only used to shame me. He takes my chin in his hand, turning me back to face him and says, "I'm worried that when you leave tonight, I'll never stop thinking about you."

Chapter Five

Suddenly, the music coming from inside the house stops and the backlights turn on. The door behind us rips open and we see Alex, Dan, and Fallon's friend, Katie. Alex and Dan are both grinning. Katie, not so much. They've been gone for just over three hours and weren't expecting to see Fallon and I talking when they got back. I fill with anger knowing that I won't get to hear the end of Fallon's thought. I'm left again with nothing. No reassurance or closure. We were inches apart a second a go and now we stand feet away from one another. My head is hung low and I'm trying to process what was just said to me, along with what's happening right now in front of us. Katie grabs Fallon's hand and pulls him inside. It's not like we did anything wrong, but she's making it seem that way.

"What was that about?" Dan asks.

"I don't know, he's your friend," I say replaying the last words he said to me over in my mind. "We were just catching up," I'm trying to add more context. I realize that the more I talk, the worse it looks.

"You guys were standing so close," Alex says using her hands to calculate the distance.

"I know," I say shaking her hands apart. "Do you know if there's anyone that can drive me home?" I ask. I feel hurt by all of this. I remember how long it took me to forget Fallon the first time. Now he's dropped this on me and isn't even sticking around to explain.

"Let me check," Alex says.

She walks back into the house and I see her fade into the crowd of people who've just returned. After a few minutes she's back, telling me that the only person who hasn't drank too much is Fallon. She says Fallon's driving Katie home now anyways, and that she only lives a town over from me.

"This is too much," I let out a breath of air, showing that I am clearly upset. I push past her and walk straight up to Fallon and Katie.

"Can we go now?" I demand.

"Yes, the car is out front," Fallon replies. Katie is staring at me. It's clear she doesn't like me. She rolls her eyes up at Fallon, giving her wordless disapproval of me tagging along.

We walk out to the car. I quickly climb into the backseat, leaving them to sit in the front. There's nothing but silence for the entire first half of the ride. Katie is anxiously tapping her knee, she looks uncomfortable. It looks like she's trying with everything inside of her not to ream Fallon out. I'm the only thing stopping her at this point. I recognize that look and I don't blame her. If she heard what he said to me thirty seconds before she walked out, she would probably be walking home right about now. I see my phone light up on the seat beside me. It's a text from Alex.

"Let me know when you're home. Thanks for coming," she writes.

I turn the phone over and rest my head on my hand that's propped up on the window. I watch Fallon driving and fall asleep gazing at his hands on the wheel.

--

When I wake up, we're stopped in front of my house. Katie is gone and Fallon is facing me. The light above him is on and his hand is brushing my shoulder, trying to gently wake me up. "Hey, we're here," he says softly.

I sit up slowly trying to grasp my surroundings. I step outside of the car, my feet planting hard on the cement below me. They want to run. However, they know they can't move again without closure. We silently walk to my door and I'm not sure why he's coming this close to my house without knowing whether or not Joey is home.

"Thanks for the drive, I think I'm okay from here," I say sharply.

I turn to go, and he grabs hold of my wrist. My bad wrist.

"Wait," he pleads.

"Fallon!" I snap. He immediately lets go, realizing he's causing me pain.

"Oh, shit! I'm so sorry, are you okay?" he asks.

"No, I'm not, but not because of that," I say holding my wrist. "What was the point in telling me all of that back there?" I take a step back. "Are you now somehow ready to have me in your life? I'm not sure if you know this, but I'm married. I have been for years now. Just because you show up in my life doesn't mean that I'll drop everything to be with you. I don't even know you!" I shout.

All of the things that I was thinking on the car ride before I fell asleep fly out of my mouth. Fallon walks up toward me, taking my hand and looking at my wedding ring. He's looking at it the same way he was looking at my bracelet earlier, as if he's surprised by something he already knows. It's like he thought I would hold off for him. For someone who never really had any intention of coming back into my life. His eyes slowly follow an invisible trail from my hands all the way up to my neck. He rests his empty hand there. I'm anxious and angry; he isn't answering any of my questions. He's just letting me yell at him, patiently waiting for the anger to pass. My mouth stops. He's close to me again, pulling me back into a trance. I can feel my anger dissolve and my heartbeat quicken. I wonder if he can hear it too. Nobody has ever had this much power over me before.

Whatever is between us feels too strong to stop. His hand trails from my neck and up into my hair, brushing it behind my ear and pulling me to meet his lips. Just like he kissed me five years ago. The same soft lips full of passion, this time with the addition of lust. We are standing outside of my house, nothing but a kiss holding us together. It feels natural. I've never forgotten what kissing Fallon is like. The heat of his breath, the velvet of his skin, the way his body feels under the fabric of his clothes. Just like that, I'm emotionally back where I started: twenty-two, lusting over an unobtainable man. I can feel that he misses me too. I can feel it in the patterns of his kiss, slow and painful. As my lips fall from his they pull sweet-tasting memories from my mind. I stand and look at him sadly trying to remember everything in this moment again. I don't want to forget the way the lights on my house light up his eyes and cast an uneven shadow on his skin. I kiss him again. This time, it's entirely from a place of lust. It's now my choice and my need for him is intensely strong. Five years of wanting someone and missing someone, transmitted through the best words I know how to use: none.

He's gentle and kind; everything that Joey is not. For a brief moment I wonder what it would be like to share this home with Fallon, with someone who cares about me. Wordlessly, we take the steps up to my front door; I open it and we enter. I've already made the decision in my mind to hold onto him for as long as I can. I want to show him so much of myself that he won't want to let go. Maybe if we do this, it will hurt less when he finally leaves again. We walk blindly through my dark house, carefully trying not to illuminate the situation. My younger self pictured this scenario so many times and now that it's finally happening, everything I thought I would do has gone out the window. The strength and resilience I thought I would be able to maintain no longer exists as we walk to my bedroom, past walls of wedding photos and belongings that clearly don't belong to me. My eyes fall to them and then up to Fallon. His eyes don't look at anything, except for me. After all, this is the life he claims he's unable to give me. It must hurt.

After a long and quiet walk to my room, I open the door and we move to my bed. He lays me down, watching me wait for him as he takes his shoes off and places them to the side. I smile at this. He's being very cautious, carefully executing all of his moves. They're smooth and premeditated. He takes off his jacket and places it along the foot of the bed.

"Come," I say, trying not to sound too desperate as he slides his pants down to his ankles and lifts his shirt from over his head.

"Are you sure this is okay?" he asks. Of course it's not, but that doesn't mean I don't want it to happen. I'm not sure how to answer his question, so I just nod.

He climbs over top of me, resting his body half on top of me and half on the bed beside me. His legs fall into place with my body, fitting naturally as if they were always meant to rest here. His fingers trail from my collarbone all the way down my thigh making me breathe heavily. His eyes are wandering over each part of me and his lips are kissing me everywhere. I'm not used to affection like this. Kiss after kiss, our bodies press closer together, repeating the same rhythms, creating friction. We're frantically grabbing each other, and we're scared to let it stop.

All of my thoughts drop in their place. My lungs feel like they've released air that's been waiting to escape since he last left, and my hands press softly into his neck. It feels like we're spinning, but I know we aren't because he's holding me strongly in place. I haven't pulled away and I don't want to. His mouth moves softly with disparity. He brings his head back for a moment and I don't look at him. I'm scared if he gives me the chance to let go, I'll make the wrong decision. Suddenly he sits up on his knees, scaling me once more. He then takes off the layers of clothes wrapped around my body. I feel like crying knowing that this might be the first and last time we're together. He breathes heavily as his hands trace me.

"You're perfect, Josephine," he lets out.

His eyes are full of warmth as he pushes into me and I push my hand into his hair, grabbing hold of his soft curls. He blindly feels the edges of my cheek, cupping my head with his hands until he opens his eyes and pushes my hair off my shoulder, tracing his thumb along my collarbone again. He doesn't stop looking at me as he moves. The way he touches me so softly... it's like he's comparing each part of me to what he previously pictured in his mind. My cheeks burn hot as I arch my back upwards, feeling bliss. I've never felt this before and that thought alone scares me. Calculating the way his eyes sway closed, I can tell he feels the same. His hands hold mine above my head and he releases a deep breath into me. Just like that, we fall back into place beside each other.

The reality of everything sets in. I lay with my back facing him, willing him to hold me. The memories from five years ago hit me quickly, and I begin to cry lightly and silently. Tears stream down the left side of my face, which he can't see. There's something stopping me from soaking in what just happened between us. It's the same thing that holds me back from enjoying anything else in life. I can't stop thinking about him.

Joey.

Joey.

Joey.

He echoes through my mind. Not in a way of regret or resentment, but in a way of worry. I'm scared of what will happen if he finds out.

"What's wrong?" Fallon asks.

"It's Joey," I say what I'm thinking.

"You don't need him," his hold tightens around me, gently pressing his lips into my hair. "You can come stay with me."

"You know I can't do that. I have my entire life here with him. He's my husband," I whisper.

I think about how easy it would be for me to just go into my closet and grab the duffel bag that I have half-packed and ready to go. I can't. I feel stuck to him. If you asked me five years ago, I would have gone with Fallon in a heartbeat. And I want to now more than anything. The things I feel for him are unexplainable, but there's something stopping me. It's fear.

Fallon suddenly gets up, putting his clothes back on. I sit up and watch. This can't be it.

"You don't get it, do you? This guy is not good for you. It kills me to think that bastard could do what he's done to you. It makes me sick. It should make you sick too. I know it does," tears now fill his eyes too; he's angry. "You know, since we met I've never dated anyone. I couldn't. I know it sounds insane, it probably is, but there's just something about you that isn't in anyone else," his voice breaks.

"Then why did you let me leave? You never called or texted me after that night. It would have been too easy for you to get my information. All the times I would hang out with Dan, he wouldn't tell me a single thing about you. He wouldn't even tell Alex when she asked. Your driver told me about your parents. I can't image what that must be like. I only know it completely devastated you because it made you put up a wall so high that nobody could get in. It hurts to watch," I say sadly.

"The reason I told you I couldn't see you didn't have anything to do with that. Yes, that's why I was crying on the balcony, but there's so much more." He pauses then continues. "I was so sad that night because I knew my mom would've loved you. If she thought a girl like you could walk into my life, she'd make me hold onto you. But she's not here. And since she left, I've had to do a lot of things I'm not proud of. I knew if I brought you into that, she'd hate me for it." His voice is full of desperation and disgust.

"Bring me into what?" I ask.

He steps closer, knowing that his answer will determine the outcome of our night together. "I-I can't tell you," he stutters. "I want to. I just can't," he stops.

"So, nothing's changed?" I ask.

"No, I'm still as fucked up as I was the night we met," he says putting his hand on his forehead. "That doesn't change the way I feel about you though."

"You just slept with me, turned my world upside down and now you're asking me to leave my husband and live with a man who doesn't even want to be with me?" I ask. The frustration is boiling over inside of me.

"I want to be with you more than anything," he says.

"But what?" I ask, helping him get to the point.

"But, there's still a lot I need to fix. You can come stay with me, or I can help you move your stuff in with Alex. I just can't be with you, Josephine. I don't want to ruin your life," he says.

I let out an obnoxious laugh. He knows he already has.

"I don't know what you want from me, or even what you want for yourself. I think it's pretty messed up for you to beg me all night to leave Joey, then confess feelings to me that don't have any foundation to them. I think you need to leave," I'm now crying.

"Is that what you want?" he asks.

No. I think.

"Because if it is, I'll go," he adds.

I nod tearfully, making the decision to stay here with Joey. To be unhappy for the rest of my life.

"Okay," he sighs, he knows I'm serious. He walks over to my bookshelf and grabs the first book he sees. "If you change your mind, just know that I won't change mine. Here's my number, if you ever need me, just call me." He thinks that I'll eventually need him to save me from Joey.

He rips a page from one of my books and writes on it. He puts the paper into the front of the book and places it back on the shelf. He then walks out of the room and I can see his shadow underneath the door. He waits a few minutes before walking down the stairs. I hear his footsteps trail through the house. The front door opens, and then closes. All I'm left with is yellow light peeking underneath the doorframe and my thoughts. I wander downstairs and watch as his car pulls out of the driveway. For the rest of the night I wonder if he made it home safely.

Chapter Six

eleven months until the wedding...

The screech of the hangers sliding along the rack is too loud for me this morning. It feels like we've been looking for hours already. The dress has to be simple, yet unique, silk and revealing. The main quality Alex is looking for is diamond studded straps. It must have that, no exceptions. I don't think she has any idea what she's actually looking for because her three requests completely contradict each other. She's wearing black jeans and her wedding shoes while walking around the store. She's the one who taught me how to shop feet first. That's when you pick your shoes, and then your outfit to match. It's an odd concept, yet we've both been doing this for as long as I can remember. I'm looking as hard as I can for something that resembles her wide-stretched vision. I can see her feet directly across from mine on the other side of the rack as she looks along with me.

"How about this one?" I ask.

I part the dresses between us and hold up a long pearl coloured dress against my body. She tilts her head and reaches out one arm to feel the fabric between her fingertips. She looks down at her feet and back up to the dress.

"Add it to the pile," she motions for the woman helping us to take it away.

She's loving every second of this. Although Alex didn't know it before, she's always been destined for marriage. It took her a long time to mature and settle down, but it was always on her path. When she and Dan first started going out, she would still go on dates with other guys and flirt relentlessly. When Dan found out he was crushed because he really loved her from the very start of their relationship. They were the same person. The only difference between them was that he knew he was in love right away and it took them breaking up for a month for her to figure it out. Before Dan, I had never even seen Alex cry over a guy. A month after their breakup, I picked her up from work and told her that we were going to win Dan back. At that point, she hadn't gone to a party in weeks and hardly showed up to our classes so I knew I had to do something. She was against it at first because she thought Dan had moved on and wouldn't want to see her. I had to explain that feelings don't work that way, that when you have a genuine connection with someone, the feelings don't just go away in a matter of months. After hours of trying to convince her, she finally came around and we decided that if she wanted to date him again, she'd have to do something big. Something like what you see in the movies.

The plan was to go to his apartment; I would buzz in and let her in with me. Then as I talked to Dan, she would set up a long trail of cards, flowers and candles leading to her on the floor below his. It was the best thing our tired, college brains could come up with. When we got there, she was really nervous. I looked at her seriously and told her not to do this unless she meant it. Dan and I had become pretty close in the months they were together. It wasn't worth her breaking his heart all over again. The night he'd finally called it off with Alex, she told him she was studying and couldn't hang out with him. Later that evening he caught her on a date with some guy from our school, so I was doing the right thing by having this conversation with her.

When I got her verbal confirmation, I turned off my car, opened the door and we headed up to the buzzer. As I went to call up, a woman walked out and held the door open for us. It was perfect. I snuck past her and into the elevator up to Dan's place. I told Alex to wait five minutes until she started her way into the building behind me. When I knocked on the door, I could hear rambled voices and music playing. The music quickly turned off and someone started unlocking the door. The door opened slightly and closed again quickly. I could hear chatter for a few more minutes until the door began to open again. It was Dan. I could tell that he was having a conversation with someone, but I wasn't sure who. When he finally opened the door he saw me and his eyes grew wide.

"Hey, Josie," he said loudly with his head poking out of the space between the door and its frame, "what are you doing here?"

He slipped his body out of the door and closed it behind him. As the door landed into place, I could briefly see the shadow of·a person out of the corner of my eye. I thought to myself that he must have been having a party and I started second guessing our plan.

"Hi, Dan. I just came by to see how you're doing. Can I come in?" I asked.

I took a step towards him and he reached his hand over to cover the door handle.

"I actually have someone over. I wish you'd called. I really can't hang out right now. Could you come back tomorrow?" he asked.

I wanted to shake him and tell him that he was an idiot if he had a girl over because of how hard Alex worked on her plan to get him back.

"Please don't tell Alex," he pleaded.

"How can I not?" I asked. "She's my best friend. And she's going to ask."

"It's not what you think, I promise," he said.

"It better be someone really important then, because you're going to let down a girl who just spent three hours doing a whole lot for you," I said turning to walk away.

"Wait, Josie. I have Fallon over. He told me he doesn't want to see you. He asked me to get you to go," I could feel hurt in his voice as he said this. *Fallon*. The name *did* hurt me.

I turned to look away from him again and in the same moment Alex turned the corner, lit up a candle and went to place it on the carpet. Her eyes met Dan's and she took a step backwards.

"Oh, hey..." she said.

"Hey, Alex. It's nice to s-" Dan began, before being interrupted by the sound of the fire alarm and water rapidly spewing from the ceiling. We all stood in shock with our hands on our heads, feeling damp hair.

"Oh my god! This can't be happening," Alex said as she took off and ran down the stairwell.

Someone had knocked over a few candles on the floor below while walking to their apartment, causing a small fire on the carpet. No serious damage was done. However, it was enough fire to set off the building's alarms. When Alex and I got outside I told her what Dan had said about Fallon. We were both pissed. She told me it was okay if I wanted to go, so I did. She made up with Dan but never got to read the cards she'd made him because the water smudged all of the writing. She told him how she felt in person instead, and he told her he felt the same. Ever since that day they were inseparable. And I was left hurt and confused.

--

I'm now standing across from Alex, shuffling through dresses. I'm thinking about Fallon and what happened a few months ago. I still haven't told Alex. I want to tell her today since it's just her and I out looking for her gown. It's her first time out looking at dresses and she's not planning on buying anything today, so she didn't tell the other bridesmaids we were going out. We walk back to the dressing room where piles of white and pink pearl dresses are hanging. There's not a soul in the shop, except Alex and I. I'm surprised that there's no one else here. We're in the middle of Toronto at 10:00a.m. and this is one of the most popular wedding dress stores in the city. Alex is skipping around the room.

"Isn't this great?" she asks, "there's no one here." She opens the fitting room door.

"Yeah, I was just thinking how weird it is that it's this quiet on a Saturday morning," I say passing her a dress.

She starts by trying on the dresses she doesn't think she'll like. She's doing this to prolong the process. She knows this moment will only happen once and she wants to make it last.

"Dan called months ago to book it out for today," she says naturally.

She's absolutely soaking up the life she lives with Dan, completely accustomed to it.

"That must have cost a fortune," I note. "Do you have the dress on yet? How does it look?"

"You tell me," she opens the door and walks out.

A beautiful white dress, soft and exposing hangs tight on her body. The back is open and it lines straight across her chest. It sits just above her knees and fades into a long trail behind her. The dress ruffles, changing from silk to white mesh fabric as it falls. It's gorgeous. It hits me in this moment that she's a completely different person than the Alex I once knew. She's glowing and in love; she's committed and honest; she's a bride. A beautiful, confident, and complete version of herself. I'm smiling at her harder than I ever have.

"You look stunning. Your mom would be so proud of you," I hug her. She's smiling too.

"I know she would. If I'm being honest though, I don't like it at all. It's too proper," she says. I laugh at the thought of this dress being considered to be proper by anyone.

She starts listing off everything wrong with the dress in comparison to what she wants.

"It needs to be more revealing, and shorter for sure. Maybe it's for the best that mom isn't here to see this. She'd have a heart attack," she laughs. "No, no, no,

Alexandra! The sleeves need to be longer. The dress should be down to the floor. Think about what your father will say, and your grandmother," Alex mocks.

Since her mom died two years ago, she's done nothing, but make light of it. Not in a malicious way by any means. The next closest person to Alex, besides Dan, was her mother. I think her ignoring her feelings has been her way of coping. Dan called me once to ask me if it's normal. Neither Dan nor I have ever lost a parent, so it's hard to know what to do to help her. I told him I think it's normal for her: she's never dealt well with pain - she chooses not to acknowledge it. I, on the other hand, think it's healthy to acknowledge pain. Once I tried bringing it up to her but she told me she didn't want to talk about it. She said when she's ready she'd come with me to see my therapist, Dr. Faye Romano. She told me that nearly a year ago.

I've been going to see Dr. Romano for years now. I usually see her twice a month. She doesn't have a connection to anyone in my life. No one accept Alex knows she exists in my world.

"Well then, she'd probably not want to see you walk down the aisle in this," I hand Alex a stunning V-cut dress with diamond stud straps and mesh sides. It has a completely open back, held together by a matching single strap crossing from one side of the mid-back to the other. The dress is pearl pink and tight fitting. Alex's mouth drops.

"I didn't see that one!" she almost yells.

"I saw it as soon as we walked in. When you were putting your heels on, I asked the lady to put it aside for you," I say.

"You sneak," she jokes. "I'm trying this on right now," she says as she walks back into the fitting room.

"It feels like forever since I saw you last. Lots has happened since then. Dan and I have been doing so much planning. It's insane how much work goes into a wedding," she says.

"Yes, I would know," I laugh. "How much do you guys have done?"

"We have the venue booked. It's the same place Dan proposed. It's beautiful. It's a building beside a creek with all glass walls so you can see the field and the water. It makes you feel like you're outside without actually having to be outside. It's perfect," she says with excitement.

She walks out of the dressing room and our conversation stops. The dress she has on is exactly what she wanted. It didn't make sense when she originally told me, but now that I can see it all melded together on her, I get it.

"That's the one," I say walking up to her.

We both stand facing the mirror. My head is over her shoulder, just staring at her reflection in awe. I can't believe this is finally happening. There's so much to plan in so little time. The wedding is in eleven months. That's eleven months to get the groom's attire, the wedding party's attire, the flowers, the catering, the entertainment and the bachelor and bachelorette parties booked. It's going to take a lot of work but I'm ready to do whatever she needs me to.

"I don't know how I am going to explain this to Dan. I told him I wouldn't buy anything," she says, still looking at herself in the dress. I can tell she's looking for ways to justify it. I think that the way she looks in the dress right now will be enough reason.

"I really don't think he'll care. He probably makes enough money to cover this in a day," I say laughing. "Remember that time we almost spent ten thousand dollars on your birthday?"

"Yeah, how could I forget that? Buying those plane tickets just to piss Dan off. I was so mad at him. That's still my favourite trip and I still wear those earrings every day," she says.

She pushes her hair back behind her ears to reveal small studded diamond earrings. We bought a matching set at Tiffany's in New York. It's one of the only things we bought the entire trip because they were three thousand dollars each. She and Dan had gotten into a huge fight over Dan's mom staying over for the week. Alex and Dan's mom have never gotten along. She thinks Alex isn't good enough for Dan and she isn't shy to admit it. The first time she met Alex's family she told them too. So when Dan invited his mom to stay over at their place on Alex's birthday, Alex called me and said we were going to New York. Not even five hours after we left Dan had already been in contact with the hotel. I had texted him the hotel's name - I couldn't keep it from him. He somehow got connected to our room's line from the front desk and he was livid. It wasn't because we had spent ten thousand dollars at his expense; it was because he wanted to know that she was safe. It's really sweet to know that Alex still wears the earrings. I'm sure she hears too much about them from Dan not to.

When she gets out of the dress, she pays for it at the front and they send for her size to be shipped to the boutique. It's a size too big and it needs to be taken in a few inches along the bottom.

"So, this is it. I'm officially a bride," she says with confusion.

"Trust me, Al, there's a lot more work to be done," I correct her.

"I know, I was just expecting this part to take a lot longer," she adds.

We head off to our next destination: breakfast. She takes me to a cafe by her work. I've never been there, but she says the pastries are to die for. She goes there almost every morning. The Steamed Bean is her version of the cafe by my house. I order an iced latte and a chocolate croissant: my staple breakfast. It's the one thing that every place has and it's really hard to mess up, even if you try. We sit in the corner by the window, the hot sun shining right on my back. The air has just started to warm, and you can see how dry everything is outside. She sits down in front of me with her peppermint latte. She always adds one sweetener, one sugar, and creamer. It's the weirdest thing I've ever heard of. Sitting next to her cup is a double toasted bagel with light cream cheese and avocado on top. She opens the bagel and takes a bite, sipping her drink to wash it down. I place a straw in my cup and stir.

"Is this made with cream?" I ask.

"Um, not sure. How would you tell?" she replies.

"Here," I say as I hold my straw to her, and she takes a sip. I've been getting better at sharing my drinks over the years. I think it's a side effect of adulthood.

107

"Just taste how thick it is. What kind of coffee shop makes their lattes with cream?" I ask.

"I think most places use cream instead of milk unless you ask," she suggests.

I nod, sipping it again. It's definitely cream. I hate cream. I've been drinking my coffee the same way for as long as I can remember. Iced, and with milk. Sugar is too sweet and cream, too thick.

"Just ask them for another one. I'm sure they won't mind," she adds.

"It's okay, I don't want to waste it," I say.

"Man, Joey's starting to rub off on you," she laughs.

She's implying that I'm picky, which I completely agree with. Over the years Joey has taught me how to get what I want and that if I ask for something, it should be done that way or not at all. I don't agree with it, however using his fixed mindset is the only way I've been able to keep up with planning his parties. All of his short timelines and demands can only be done by being uptight and picky.

"Enough about my coffee, we have some important things to discuss," I say.

I pull a binder out of my bag. On the front "Alex's Wedding" is printed in large cursive font. She stares intently.

"What is that?" she asks.

"It's your wedding planner," I reply, opening the book.

There's a table of contents on the first page. Page's one through four are for venue, colour, and scheme. Pages four through seven are for the guest list, followed by budgeting, then caterers, bachelorette party planning, and a month-to-month outline of things that will be needed. You name it, it's in there.

"This is so beautiful," she gasps, flipping through the pages and pressing her fingers onto the fabrics.

There are sections with my own ideas, colours and fabrics that I've seen and thought would suit her vision. There's also space for her to put her own ideas. She's been planning this wedding for a lot longer than Dan knows about. I took mental note of this, and any time I would find something that matched I would add it to the book. Since I'm not really working anymore, I've had a lot more free time and needed something to keep my passions alive.

"It's nothing; you know I love this kind of stuff. I knew this would happen eventually. Dan and I actually went ring shopping for you once a year ago," I boast.

She hates it when I don't tell her stuff. She rolls her eyes at me and laughs. We start putting down names on her guest list, considering she already has her venue set. We jot down the wedding party, her dad, Dan's parents, their grandparents, uncles, aunts, and friends.

"Is Joey going to come?" she asks.

"Of course, you know he wouldn't miss it," I answer. I am a bit offended that she's even asking.

"I'm just worried. You know, because of what happened last time we saw him... I don't want anything like that to happen again," she says looking away from me.

The last time Dan and Joey were in the same room together they almost killed each other. Joey was drunk and said something nasty about Dan's line of work. He basically said that there's no way Dan could make more than he does just from his pilot salary. He was implying that Dan gets his money another way. It was out of line and it took weeks for Dan to even talk to us after that night. At one point, Joey grabbed Dan by the collar of his shirt and that's when Alex asked us to leave. Joey can't control his jealousy and it almost cost me my two best friends.

"Don't worry, he's over it. I promise I'll keep him in line," I say smiling, uncertain if I'm even capable of controlling Joey.

We finish up our breakfast and she asks me if I have any ideas for her bachelorette party.

"I was thinking Piper's Peak. It's in the hills about an hour from your place. It's one of those Scandinavian spas on a huge private property. It's big enough that Dan could come with the guys and we wouldn't even see each other. There's even a small club on the property," I say trying to convince her. Partly because I know she would love it, and partly because I wanted to go when I was getting married. Joey wanted Vegas. He won that argument.

"That sounds perfect. Dan will be so impressed with me roughing it," she laughs.

"Oh my god, Al! You're going to be staying at a five-star resort with full showers and electricity. There's nothing about this place that remotely suggests you'll be roughing it," I shake my head at her.

We talk about all of the plans she has in mind for a few hours. We sip our second coffees down to the bottom of our cups, picking away at the flakes left from my croissant. A look of discomfort crosses her face. The same look she had when she told me that Fallon is in the wedding party. I realize again that I haven't told her about what happened between us. It's not like I haven't been thinking about it. It's on my mind all the time. It makes my stomach twist with guilt. I think I'll wait until after the wedding; I'm still having enough trouble getting past it on my own.

"I know things were kind of crazy at my party and I haven't seen you since to talk about it," she says. "But Fallon's been by the house."

She's insinuating that there's something she knows; I know she's bluffing. If she had any clue what happened between us she would have been at my house the next morning. She pauses for a while, giving me room to fill in the blanks and when she realizes I am not going to bite she continues. "He said that he didn't want to talk about it, which doesn't surprise me. He's just been in a really horrible mood since then," she says glaring at me.

"There's not much to talk about, we were just catching up. Hashing some things out from the past," I stir my straw into the melting ice cubes and sip its contents.

"So, I guess It's not going to be a problem planning the parties then?" she asks, raising an eyebrow.

"What parties?" I say bluntly.

"Well, it was your idea to do the bachelorette party and the bachelor party at the spa, so you'll probably need to coordinate with each other..." she stops.

I tell her it's fine and that I'm sure I can email and tell him when we're going to go and what he'll need to do. She seems content with that and doesn't ask any more questions. Something about this conversation feels unfinished.

--

I walk through the front door of my house and I'm left exhausted. I drop my purse down on the floor beside me and a loud thud follows. The house is quiet because Joey isn't home. He's at his second conference this week. He's been in a great mood lately; talkative and full of energy. Though he's been happy, I'm also relieved to be home alone. I mostly sleep on the couch these days. I haven't been able to sleep in my bed since Fallon was here; I usually wake up in a panic. I dream about the night of the party and it always ends up the same: with me sitting by the window, watching the taillights of his car flashing into my eyes. Since I sleep talk, it's not safe for me to be in the same bed as Joey. He doesn't think much of this because he's usually only home once a week. When he isn't out of town, he spends most of his nights at the hospital. The nights he's home, he doesn't pester me about my absence. He's stuck in a haze, a haze that will eventually break.

He'll be starting at the hospital in Washington next summer or when they find someone who can replace him here. As of right now, the date sits as June 1st. We've been talking about moving there because he really likes the idea of not having to travel far. Besides, he doesn't have a lot of family in Canada. The thought of leaving my family behind presses on my chest, a weight too heavy to lift. I still haven't told him whether or not I'm okay with the move and he hasn't asked me.

The pizza that I ordered on my way home has just arrived. One large cheese, with cheese sauce. I haven't had it since I was a kid and I'm feeling nostalgic tonight. I take the box and light some candles. I like being in the dark. It feels comforting and warm. I sit in my reading chair by the window, picking at the bits of cheese as it cools while I read. Just to my left is a half-bottle of chardonnay from this week. If Joey were here, I would never leave it out like this. He doesn't like me drinking when he's not here. He says I am too unpredictable. I don't care what he says, the wine has been helping me sleep and he's not here to stop me. It starts to rain as I turn through my book while eating my dinner, alone and content. I stare at the raindrops as they trickle down the window. This weather makes me happiest. My eyes are stuck on one drop of water, my lips sipping wine and my mind is hazy. As the raindrop hits the bottom of the window my phone buzzes. It startles me, but I drop my hand down to the table to pick it up.

"Save my number under the name Jennifer and then delete this," I read. What the hell? Who is this? I unlock my phone and stare at this message. I see three dots flash across the bottom left of the screen. This person is still typing... Maybe they have the wrong number.

Before I let them finish and disclose any more information, I send a message, "Wrong number."

"It's not; we have a mutual friend that says we have some planning to do. Meet me at 347 Gateway Avenue tomorrow at 8:00a.m.," they reply.

My first thought is Alex. The only planning I have to do right now is for her wedding. It feels like she's trying to set me up into meeting Fallon again. Then I remember that he left his phone number in one of my books. I race upstairs, almost knocking the pizza off the table beside me. My feet move fast up the stairs and into my bedroom. My hands shuffle quickly around my bookshelf and pull out the book, "One Last Chance," one of many romance novels written by my favourite author. I flip to the first page, where the folded paper is resting. I open it, pass my fingers along the writing and compare it to the corresponding number above the text. It's him. If Joey was here and he had seen my phone light up attached to a message like that... I can't bring myself to finish that thought. A chill shoots through my body, but I find myself complying anyways.

I reply, "OK," and delete the message.

I walk back to my chair, slide another piece of pizza into my mouth and open my book. I know I will fall asleep like this again, so I set my alarm for 7:00a.m. and mark the location Fallon sent me in my calendar.

Chapter Seven

It's 7:45a.m., the busiest time of the day for coffee
making. My fingers are rattling along my steering wheel
anxiously.

"If meeting with Fallon is making you this nervous,
maybe it's not such a good idea," Dr. Romano echoes
through the speaker of my phone. She's the only person
I've been completely honest with and she's probably
right. I've been talking to her for so long now that her
opinion heavily influences me. She's someone who will
always give me their honest opinion, an opinion that I
pay a lot of money for.

"It feels weird. I'll get over it though," I say shaking my nerves out. "You were the one who told me that I need come to terms with my past. It's the one thing in my life that's kept me from moving forward," I state.

"You're right. I think closure is just what you need and I'm glad you're doing this. Just hold your ground, ask all of the questions you can think of, and don't hesitate to leave if it's too much. This is the next step in moving forward. You need this," she comforts me.

"Thanks, Faye, I'll call you later," I say hanging up the phone.

I called her the day after Fallon was at my house. She told me that if we left things the way we did last time, in five more years I'll still wonder what went wrong. *We can be just friends,* I repeat in my mind. *We are friends planning a wedding. Just two strangers helping each other for a few months and then we can put all of this behind us. I can focus on my marriage and he can focus on whatever is happening in his world. It's going to be simple.*

I pull up in front of the cafe and I'm early. My entire body is full of angst despite my conversation with Faye. Rushes of confusion filter through me and I'm tense.

"I can do this," I say to myself.

I let out a deep breath and open my car door. I step on a branch as I get out and it cracks beneath my feet. There couldn't be a more perfect metaphor for what I'm feeling right now. The walk from my car to the cafe is comfortable, as it always is on my routine visits, but this time it isn't routine. It is the exact opposite. I wonder if Fallon feels the same way. If you had told me five years ago that I would be on my way to have small talk in a coffee shop with Fallon Adams, I wouldn't believe you.

I push the door to the cafe open and it's very busy. There's a loud hum of noise from every corner of this place. It fills my ears. I know right now that I will not be able to get anything done in a place this noisy. I haven't noticed the noise before today. I walk up to the cash register to wait in line. There's only one person ahead of me. I look straight to the back of the shop and my eyes find Fallon sitting behind a computer. He's wearing glasses today and they suit his face perfectly. He's gripping a pen that is scribbling down thoughts. He looks normal. Not normal enough to go unnoticed; the type of normal that attracts every eye in the room. Anxiety fills me again and I think how it's strange seeing him like this. He's probably never been here before, yet I feel like I just stepped into his world. He couldn't blend in if he tired. In a crowd of people, he's far from ordinary. He takes his hand and pushes his hair back. A curl falls in front of his face and he moves it with his pen. I breathe heavily again.

"I can do this," I repeat.

"Miss?" the cashier is trying to get my attention.

"Oh!" I jump. "Sorry, an iced latte and a chocolate croissant please."

"Sounds good, medium right?" she pauses. "You order the same thing most of the time, I didn't want to guess and get it wrong," she laughs awkwardly.

I nod, looking back over to Fallon. He hasn't even noticed me. He's entirely in his own world. I'm fifteen minutes early yet I'm still late. I wanted to get here first so I could sit and establish myself in my own territory and Fallon could be the one who feels uncomfortable. I pick up my coffee and make my way to the table.

"Josephine," he says as he lifts his head. "It's nice to see you." He stands up and hugs me. It's short side-hug. He smells so nice. A wave of memories punches me in the gut. I need to stop.

"Hi, can I sit?" I ask.

"Of course," he says pulling my chair out and sitting back down.

"Thanks for coming. I figured it would be best to meet in person after... How things went last time," he takes a breath tilting his head. I enjoy seeing the discomfort he feels as he recalls our night together.

"I met with Alex yesterday. It sounds like there's a lot that she's expecting us to do together. I don't want to let her down, but I think we need to talk first," I say with unease.

"I couldn't agree more," he says reaching for his briefcase and pulling out a thin portable printer with some paper. I've never seen one so small before.

"Do you carry that thing around everywhere with you?" I mock.

"Yes, it's for work. You never know when it will come in handy," he says.

"What are you going to print?" I'm now curious. I don't understand why a pilot needs to carry around a printer.

"I'm glad you ask," he pauses. "The first order of duty on my list as Dan's best man is to establish boundaries," he says looking up at me, eyes peering over his glasses. "Because no matter how much I want to kiss you right now, I can't. As we established already, you are not willing to leave Joey and I can't expose you to my life. So we need a formal agreement and I figured that's what we could do today," he stops.

"Fallon!" I say loudly, looking over my shoulder to see if anyone heard him. He's so blunt. He just says what's on his mind. I'm shocked and I'm not doing a good job at hiding it.

"What?" he laughs, filling his mouth with a piece of my chocolate croissant.

"Okay, fine. Let's get started because my first rule is no more saying you want to kiss me," I say as I roll my eyes.

"I'll add that, but I think the first place to start is by wiping the slate clean. Getting out any questions we both might have," he clicks a new tab open on his laptop. "We hadn't seen each other for a long time before Alex and Dan's party. I know I have some questions and I'm sure you do too."

"One question," I say.

"What do you want to know?" he asks.

"No, I mean we only get one question each. I have work in about two hours," I lie.

I just don't want this to take all day. I have some errands to run for Joey's birthday party. He's going to be home tonight from working a two-day shift. I don't want to give him a reason to ask me about where I was today. The look on Fallon's face shows me he knows I'm full of shit but he doesn't say anything about it.

"Agreed. I need a minute to come up with mine though," he says.

"Okay, let me know when you're ready," I reply.

We're silent for a few minutes. My discomfort begins to fade away and suddenly we are back to normal. The anticipation leading up to seeing him always makes me nervous, it's as though I forget how comfortable he makes me feel once we begin our bantering. I watch him think, since I already know my question.

My mind starts to drift. I'm so surprised with how well he's aged. It's only been five years, but he looks almost the same.

He finally says he's ready, so I nod at him to go first.

"My question is about the bruises," he says.

"The bruises? Listen Fallon, I can take care of that on my own. I don't need to talk to you about it," I answer feeling defensive and embarrassed.

"You agreed to one question. That's my question and I'm not changing it," he says sincerely. I rub my thumb on the spot of my arm that was once purple and blue. Pulling the sleeve of my shirt over top of it.

"I know the last time we spoke we left on a really bad note," he continues. "I came here today to ask you this exact question so please just answer it. Everything happened so quickly at the party, I didn't have time to think. I just saw your wrist and I couldn't control myself. After I left you there that night, I haven't been able to get the thought of you being hurt by him out of my head. I know that you haven't told Alex because you wouldn't still be living there," he says letting out a breath.

"It's not going to happen again. Joey is barely home. He's around maybe once a week and we're better than we have been in years. I think it was just a one-time thing," I say. "I appreciate your concern and I'm sorry that you had to see me like that, but I promise that I won't let it get out of hand further than it has."

"How do you know he's changed? It's only been a few months since he hurt you," he says.

"We've been married for three years; I know my husband," I say sternly.

"If you say so. Now what's your question?" he asks. He knows there's nothing more he can say.

"The only thing I want to know is what's so wrong with you? Why haven't you ever been in a relationship?" I ask.

"That's two questions. Which is it?" he replies.

"I just want to know what it is that makes you unlovable. You told me the night we met that there's something about you that makes you unable to commit. There's this big secret in your life that you always fail to elaborate on. You just use the excuse of not wanting to subject me to your life," my face is getting hot - there's a bit of anger behind this question. "Honestly, not that it's my place, but I think it's your parents' death that makes you feel this way. You're using it as a way to push people out. You have to know that it's not your fault that they aren't here anymore." I'm staring at him with pain in my eyes.

"Do you even know how they died?" he asks.

"No, you've never told me," I say.

"Then please don't say that to me ever again," he says.

He isn't looking at me anymore because he's trying not to cry.

"The reason I push people away doesn't have anything to do with my parents. You asked me this last time I saw you. Do you have another question you wanted to ask?" he says.

I can tell he's angry at me but he's trying not to show it.

"I don't have any other questions," I say softly. I shouldn't have said anything.

"Let's just move on," he suggests, trying to lighten the mood. "First rule, no personal questions."

I nod and he writes it down.

--

We go back and forth making up rules for each other. I'm having a lot of fun if I'm being honest. I can tell he is too. The next three rules are no physical contact, no seeing each other unless it pertains to the wedding, and absolutely nobody outside of the wedding party can know that we're meeting.

"Did you move up here to be by this coffee shop?" is the next thing he says to me.

"No more personal questions, remember?" I smirk.

After his last comment I don't think I can handle anything strictly other than business.

"Fair enough," he says.

He whips his laptop around to face me. Its screen is showing pictures of the lodge I mentioned to Alex.

"Looks nice, I think we should book it a month from the wedding. That way everyone will be hyped up," he adds.

I agree. He seems to have all of the same interests when it comes to planning the wedding. It's nice to have someone to talk to who actually lets me share my opinion. Someone who agrees with me on things without a fight. For the next half an hour before I have to go, we talk about the bachelor and bachelorette parties. I book connecting rooms for the girls and he books connecting rooms on the opposite side of the lodge for the guys. Once we're finished he packs his laptop away and we walk out of the coffee shop together. My heart begins to ache as we approach yet another goodbye. It always feels final, although I know I will see him again soon. We shake hands and walk our separate ways. When I get to my car, I start it and head to a caterer to test and order food for Joey's party.

--

When I get home the sun is just setting over the sky. Peach pink lights the corners of my home. I love the way it looks. As I begin cooking, I feel light and airy. I'm making chicken Alfredo with a homemade sauce and the house smells great. I just want Joey to get home so I can tell him about my day. In that same moment, I remember that I can't. The headlights of his car reflect through the window, contrasting against the pink sky. He's home. I take off my apron and straighten myself out. He's the type to notice if my mind is a mess based on my appearance. I practice a few smiles before his key twists in the door.

I pull the door open and embrace him, kissing his lips hard. He's taken back by this.

"It's so nice to have you home," I say with a shaky voice.

"Hey, love, nice to be back. I've had the longest week," he says as he lets go of me. I take his suitcase and head upstairs to put it away for him.

"Just get settled in, I'm making you dinner. When I come back down let's have some wine and you can tell me all about work," I yell down to him.

"Sounds good. Just leave my suitcase up there, I'll unpack it today. And better make my wine a scotch," he replies.

In all our years of being married he's never unpacked his own suitcase. My heart is pounding. Joey is a man of many things, but consistency and order are at the top of the list. I can't do anything except comply: I have to leave the bag. I turn and walk downstairs. The airiness I felt is gone and the sun has set. I pour him a glass of scotch over ice and kiss behind his neck. He smells different. Something is wrong.

I sit and talk to Joey about his days of working and his two-day trip across the border. He's full of life... I've never seen him like this before. He talks about how excited he is to move and start a life in America. I sip my wine and nod along with him but all I can think about is the suitcase. What's inside of it?

Dinner goes by fast. I can't remember anything he's said to me in the last thirty minutes. I'm staring at his smile and thinking about how I know nothing about this man at all. I feel sadness knowing I can't ever question him about it either. I'm scared to find out what would happen if I did. There's a strangeness inside of me thinking about the possibility that he has been unfaithful. I tell myself I'm a hypocrite. This is all my fault.

"I've missed you, Josie," he says interrupting my thoughts. He never calls me Josie. I smile at him. "Now clear up the table. I need to go take a shower." He kisses my forehead and walks off, cutting our conversation short.

I pile the dishes in my arms and clean up. I grab my phone off of the counter and open it. An email notification awaits me. The subject reads, "Wanted to make sure you got a copy," from someone named Jennifer Smith. I open the attachment. It's the list I made today with Fallon. I let out a smile. A real smile this time.

Chapter Eight

nine months until the wedding...

There are about twenty people in our house right now putting up temporary walls and rolling in large blackjack tables and slot machines. The place is really coming together for Joey's party tonight. Joey is upstairs in his office working. He's been working from home for the past three days and is also taking off the next two days. He has high expectations for the party tonight, yet he hasn't helped out with a single thing. In his opinion, he's helping if he passes me his cheque book. I've been planning this party for months and I'm excited to finally see Alex. She's picking me up in five minutes to go and get Joey's birthday gift from the dealership.

I start walking upstairs to say goodbye to Joey. I weave in and out of the mess of our home. Our house is huge, four stories tall·and completely open concept. However, with the space being occupied by the movers, caterers, and our decor staff it looks stuffy. My knuckles lightly tap the office door.

"Come in," Joey replies.

"Hey, I'm just going out with Alex to pick up a few extra things for the party," I say looking at the clock above his desk for the time. "You should start getting ready in about an hour. Our guests will be arriving at seven thirty and I might not be back in time."

"You're going to get the car, right?" he looks up at me. "Because the garage has been finished for weeks and it will be upsetting if I show it to my colleagues and it's empty," he says sternly. His words come off as a warning.

"Yes," I say lightly. "You can't keep anything a surprise," I add trying to joke with him.

"When you've been married to someone for as long as we've been, there's no room for secrets," he replies. He says this as if three years is a century.

He spins his chair around and reaches for my hand. I take it, moving closer to him and placing myself on his lap.

"Tonight is going to be amazing," he says into my ear.

The hairs on my neck stand. He brushes over them with his free hand and firmly grips my neck.

"I have invited your friends from Alex's wedding. I wanted to do something nice for you," his grip slowly gets harder. My breathing starts to quicken.

"Joey, you're hurting me," I start before he interrupts me.

"Listen to me," he says with anger. My eyes swell. I don't understand him. *I don't understand us.* How can he shift so quickly in emotion? "Since I've done this for you, I'm expecting you to be on your best behaviour. I have my colleagues and closest friends coming tonight, I don't need any shit from you and your friends. Understand?" he stops.

"Okay," I say as my eyes blink out tears. I hear our doorbell ring and jump up. He releases his grip and I wipe my face. "It's Alex, I have to go."

Joey turns around and picks up his glasses, placing them back on his face, and continues his work without missing a beat. I close the door softly and run down the stairs. My tears break through and flow helplessly down my face. I open the door with red eyes.

"Alex!" I say, throwing my arms around her, partly because I miss her and partly because I don't want her to see me cry.

"These are for you," she says handing me a bottle of wine and flowers. White calla lilies, my favourite.

"Thanks, hon," I smile.

I turn from her and put them on the counter. This is the first time our countertops have seen flowers bought by someone other than me in years.

"Ready to go? I left my car running out front," she says.

I grab my purse and we take off. Alex drives us to the dealership. I've already paid for the car, a red Tesla Model X. The week after his birthday last year we sat and put in the order.

Alex and I are now sitting in the lobby, waiting for the car to be brought out. She can tell something is off.

"What's up? You haven't said more than ten words since we left the house," she says sipping her coffee.

"I just got into an argument with Joey. I'm sorry. I appreciate you coming out with me, it just caught me off guard," I reply.

"Don't take him too seriously, he's always been kind of a dick," she says. Over the years she's become less and less tolerant of him.

"I know…" I say trailing off. "He told me he invited some of our friends tonight," I'm trying to steer the conversation away from Joey.

"Oh yeah, he asked me a few weeks ago if I wanted to invite my wedding party. He said that since you've been spending a lot of time with my bridesmaids that it would be nice for him to meet them," she raises her eyebrows at me.

I purse my lips together, laughing silently. We both know that isn't true. I've been spending time with a certain individual from the wedding party and it's neither her, nor one of her friends.

"You never told me that you and Fallon were hanging out," she says smiling.

"We aren't hanging out, we've just been meeting up every few weeks to talk logistics for the bachelor and bachelorette parties," I say coolly, trying to hide my emotions. She can read me too well.

"Nice," she smirks. "You know he's into you, right?" she asks.

"Actually, yes. I do," I say. "Don't worry, we talked about everything from the past and we're just friends. We even made an agreement."

"I don't even want to know what you mean by that," she laughs. "All I know is that it's impossible for two people who have a history like you do to be just friends."

--

We arrive back at the house. I'm driving Alex's car and she's driving Joey's. It looks incredible, which is why I'm too scared to drive it. I tried, but my hands shook each time I put them on the wheel. If I messed this up for him, he'd never forgive me. Alex parks it at the charging station in the new section of the garage.

"The garage looks amazing," she says closing the car door. "You've done such a good job. Joey must be so happy," she smiles at me. It *does* look amazing, but there's nothing I could do that would impress him anymore.

The sun has set, and the outside lights are turning on. The guests have already arrived, they're all inside. I can hear the music echo through the walls of the garage. We walk through the door, into the back hall and up the winding staircase that leads to the top floor, just outside of my bedroom. Alex and I still need to get ready. I'm sure Joey isn't going to be happy that I wasn't here to greet the guests. I grab my dress from my closet. It's all black and silk with a slit on its left side. Alex just happens to be wearing the same exact one in blue. We planned this last week. Well, she planned it by ordering them online and shipping one to my house. She reaches into her suitcase where it lays half unpacked on the floor and takes out a small bottle of vodka. My serious face cracks into a laugh as she holds two shot glasses in her other hand. I snatch one from her.

"Let's pour a shot to the birthday boy," she says. "Screw him for making you smile less in life," she starts. She raises her brows as if for me to continue.

"Okay," I say as I think. "Screw him for not trying to have a friendship with you and Dan!" I stand up, feeling empowered.

"And a huge fuck him for not appreciating all of the work you've put into today!" she shouts back.

We're now left laughing relentlessly. We've both taken three shots and are lying across my bed with our hands holding our stomachs.

"Hey, can I ask you something?" she says to me.

"Yes, anything," I quickly reply.

"You'd tell me if there as anything going on with Joey, right?" she asks.

"Obviously..." I say. "Why would you ask me that?"

"I just feel like I haven't seen you in such a long time. The way that Joey snapped at Dan… I've never been able to shake it. He knows how much Dan and I mean to you and he didn't really seem to care. It made me worry that if he could snap that way at strangers, what's stopping him from doing it to you?" she says as her body shakes. A chill has run through her. "Sorry, I know I'm probably just tipsy, I don't mean to overstep."

"Alex, I would tell you," I say holding her hand. I'm trying to reassure her that nothing is going on. At the same time, I'm trying to reassure myself. She smiles at me again and nods.

"We should go down now," she says lightly. We link arms and trail out of the bedroom. As soon as our bodies go through the frame of the door we can hear the pumps of music and humming voices. The house is full of people as far as we can see.

"I never realized how big your house is," she says looking over the ledge.

As we look around the room from above, our eyes simultaneously land on Dan and Joey. It's too hard to read their faces from up here but we look at each other and our feet begin to move. As we rush down the staircase a few of Joey's friends try to stop me. I smile and keep moving. We burst into the area where Dan and Joey are standing, looking a bit frazzled and out of place.

"Hey there!" I say loudly.

"Hey, babe," Joey says as he takes his fingers and fixes my hair. Dan does the same for Alex. Only Dan follows with a kiss on Alex's cheek and Joey whispers, "you're late," into my ear.

I smile up at him apologetically and he nods. Then we all come back together.

"So, how are things going? Are you enjoying the party?" I ask. My mind is racing. I am wondering what led them to speak to one another. I know that Alex is wondering the same thing. Dan's first to answer my question.

"It looks incredible. I don't know how you always pull these parties off. It looks better than the casino in here," he smiles at me.

"Yes, it looks nice," Joey adds. "I can't wait to take my friends into the garage and hopefully show them my new car." He says this as if he's asking a question: he wants to know if I brought the car home in one piece.

"Everything's all set and ready to go. I hope you love it," I say brushing his shoulder.

"I'll let you know. I'm going to go show the heads of my department around the house and then I'll check it out. Actually, I think I'll grab some food first to hold me off until dinner. Excuse me," he replies. He pulls his arm out from around my waist, vanishing into the crowd of people.

"Yup, he's a douche," Dan says. I don't reply; I know he's not trying to be mean. In fact, I completely agree with him. Joey's so bluntly obnoxious it makes it difficult to take his side.

"I bet that introduction was fun. Sorry we weren't here to buffer it," I say to Dan.

"It wasn't too bad; we were only talking for a few minutes actually. He was just asking me about your friend Jennifer," he says. "I know that none of us know a Jennifer, but we talked about her as if she was your and Alex's best friend in the whole wide world," he laughs.

"Thanks, Dan," I look up at him, thankful that he'd cover for me.

"So, who's Jennifer? You better not have a new best friend," Alex says with a look of confusion crossing her face.

"Jennifer is Fallon. We've been meeting up to work on your wedding planning and he's been texting me under that name. You guys know Joey would freak out if he knew," I answer her. The words sound insane as I hear them said out loud. The biggest smile lines both Alex and Dan's faces.

"It's nothing: we've established boundaries and made an agreement. So you two can quit while you're ahead," I add.

"I'm not even going to pretend I know what you mean by that. All I know is that you two are made for each other. I'm gonna go get us some drinks," Dan says, turning to walk away.

"Funny, that's what Alex said earlier," I laugh, "have fun."

"Does Joey even have any idea how much work this must have taken you?" Alex asks, completely glossing over the mention of Fallon. I'm sure she'll ask her own questions later.

"He's not really home to see any of the planning. It's not his fault," I reply. Defending him makes my mouth taste salty and bitter. "How about we steer clear of him tonight? This house is big enough for us to go all night without running into him?" What a horrible thing to say about your own husband. The truth is that I know I can't avoid him all night, so I don't feel too bad about saying it.

"You read my mind," Alex says.

"Ladies," Dan says returning with two flutes of champagne.

"Thank you," I say grabbing one of the cups. "Oh, Al, what time are the girls coming?"

"They should be here any minute. My sisters are so excited to see you, and you haven't met Abigail yet. You'll love her," she says.

"I think Jade is coming too," Dan adds. I stare in confusion because I have no idea who those names belong to.

"New additions to the wedding party," Alex says filling the void.

"Charlie begged me to let Jade come. We've known her as long as we've known you and he said it would be unfair not to include her," Dan says, and I suddenly realize who she is.

"Wait, Charlie's still dating her?" I say. She's the little blonde girl who spilled her drink on me. I laugh again.

"Not sure I'd say dating, but they're still in each other's lives. She's pregnant you know," he says.

"No. Are you serious?" I say feeling my eyes widen.

The last thing in the world that guy needs is a baby. Ever since he dropped out of school he's been living off of Fallon with no end in sight. That's from what Alex has told me.

"They're a mess. She's the only consistent thing in his life and she isn't even that consistent. They break up every other month and it's hard to keep track," Dan says sipping his drink.

"I thought he'd be the last one to have a baby out of our friends," I say.

"I thought the same thing," Alex agrees.

"Speak of the devil," Dan gestures to the door.

I faintly see the top of the door open and a crowd flow in. It's hard to see them with all of these people here. I see four girls walk in, accompanied by Charlie. Two of which I don't recognize, the other two are Alex's identical twin sisters, Emily and Jessica. Trailing behind them is Fallon. He's stumbles around and then grabs a table. As I focus in on him, I can see that he's drunk. I'm not too surprised that he's here; he's part of the wedding party after all. For some reason though, his presence always sends chills through me. We start walking over to the blackjack table to meet them.

Alex and Dan sit with Charlie and the dealer starts to shuffle. I stay standing with my eyes watching Fallon walk around aimlessly. He makes his way past the people using the slot machines, then past the caterers who are lined up and serving food and walks right up to the bar. He finds a chair and sits. I watch him order a shot and take it. Then he orders another and drinks that one. He now has two lined up, ready to go. This mess of a man that I'm watching intently is drastically different from the one I've been meeting at the cafe. I stand watching Fallon pick up the dark brown shot and stare at it. He stirs it around in his hand and then sips it. I need to stop this.

"You okay?" I message him.

I watch as his hand leaves his drink and reaches into his jacket pocket. He places his phone onto the table and uses his finger to browse through it. I watch his head sway back, as if my text is causing him stress. It looks like he's typing something lengthy. The three dots flash at the bottom left of my screen for a few minutes only to be followed by a thumbs-up symbol. Part of me feels like he doesn't even know he's at my house right now. I turn to tap Alex's shoulder.

"Hey," I say as she looks up at me. Dan is tentatively holding his cards and pursing his lips. "Is something going on with Fallon? He's been here for less than twenty minutes and he's had four shots. I think he might have been wasted when he got here..."

"Oh god," she says jumping up, completely ignoring my question. She drops her cards on the table and grabs Dan. "Dan, we forgot the date," her voice is raising. "You need to get Fallon out of here!"

She's in a panic. This is causing me to panic too. Dan stands up, still holding his cards and runs across the room. He quickly sits, throwing his arm over Fallon's shoulder. I watch him order a drink as they begin talking.

"What's going on?" I ask.

"I completely forgot, I'm such an idiot. We shouldn't have come here with him. What was I thinking?" she asks. I grab her shoulder and shake. My heart is beating fast.

"What is going on?" I repeat my question, my body full of angst.

"It's the anniversary of the date Fallon's parents were killed. I completely forgot. We should have paid more attention, we've just been so busy with the wedding it slipped my mind," she rambles.

She's speaking quickly talking about him as if he were her child. My mind plays back her wording. She said his parents were *killed*? My body is overtaken by goose bumps. I feel like I've just crawled out from a deep freeze. My mind falls blank and Alex continues talking in the background.

"Al, what do you mean, killed?" I say softly, staring at Dan and Fallon in the distance. My heart is sinking into the floor.

"Oh, hon," she sighs. "I thought he'd told you... His parents were killed the year before we met Dan and Fallon," she starts.

It's so loud all around us. It hardly feels like the place to be having this type of conversation. This is one of the only places we can stand while keeping an eye on Fallon. I now understand the sense of responsibility that Alex feels over him tonight. Dan's with him now though. I'm sure he can handle Fallon for a few minutes.

"Come," she says pulling my arm. We walk over to the booths lined around the outside of the room. I slip onto the purple velvet cushion. Alex slides in beside me.

"Do you remember when my dad came to visit campus during our second year of college?" she starts. I nod in reply. "He kept talking about this huge restaurant chain that let go of a bunch of people in London. Apparently, my dad knew all about it because he sold produce to the owners. Anyways, he told us that one of the employees was so upset over being let go, that he went to the owner's house and murdered them in the middle of the night. It was all over the news for years after it happened. You must remember seeing it," she stops. A sinister feeling takes over. I blink out tears; I know where this is going.

"Those were Fallon's parents?" I ask.

"Yeah, they were," she sighs. Her words move slowly. They hold so much weight to them.

"Fallon told me about it the year I met Dan on the anniversary date. He and Dan had come home that night from the bar and Fallon was wasted. I could barely understand him. He told me that his parents had to close one of their locations due to health code violations. He said the claims weren't legitimate. That some guy had problems with his dad outside of the business and tried to sabotage him as a warning. Fallon's parents had to comply, and they weren't planning to reopen another location in that area. They had to let go of all the staff, including a guy who worked there for fifteen years. The guy completely lost it. That night he somehow got past their security gates and into the house. Fallon had been out at a bar for his friend's birthday and by the time he came home he was completely intoxicated. Fallon told me he was awake when it all happened and that he was too drunk to do anything. He heard the guy walking up the stairs and somehow pressed the emergency button on his cellphone. He just lay the phone down by his side and silently listened to the man walk into his parents' room. He said he just lay there frozen. He couldn't move, even after the guy left. He lay in the same spot when the police came and he didn't move as his parents were carried away. He said he recognized the guy who did it, so he didn't have to spend long at the station; the guy admitted to it right away. A few days after it all happened, Fallon got a call saying that the police reviewed the security footage from the front of the house and saw that Fallon had accidentally left the gate open. He hates himself for it and he tells me that every year. He says what happened paralyzed him. I think in more ways than one," she sips her drink, finishing it. Her eyes are full of tears and so are mine.

"I don't know what to say," I reply. I feel like I'm going to throw up.

"It's okay. I don't either, I never do. The way I lost my mom isn't comparable. He's acting this way because it's the only time he lets himself feel anything. There's no talking him out of it, we just let him be. It's the only day in the whole year that I see him grieve. The handful of times I've seen him cry have always been on this day. He's holding onto so much guilt," she says wiping her eyes.

"He must know it's not his fault," I whisper. "I guess that explains why he got so upset when I brought them up."

"Trust me, I've tried telling him it's not his fault. Anyways, we should get him out of here," she says.

"I think socialization might be good for him; that's what helped you when your mom passed," I suggest.

"Fallon and I are very different people. I've tried talking to him about it and he won't listen," she says sadly.

"Thanks for telling me," I say. I feel like I understand why he is the way he is now. He needs help, but he won't let people in.

Alex shakes it off as if we never even had the conversation as Fallon approaches. His eyes are red, and they blink slowly.

"Hey, you," he says pointing at me.

His hair has fallen over his face. I want badly to cup his face in my hands and tell him I understand so much more now. I see Joey in the background with a group of his friends and the feeling vanishes from my mind.

"Hey, Fallon, I'm really happy you came," I try not to sound desperate.

"Fallon and I were just about to hit the slots. Do you girls want to join?" Dan asks.

"I'll come. I brought a few hundred with me and I can feel it burning in my pocket," Alex says.

"I should go check on Joey and get the food ready to go," I say. I lean in and hug Fallon, squeezing him in with the same sideways hug he gave me at the cafe.

"No touching, remember?" he says, shooting a wink at me.

He hands me his drink and walks off. I feel the condensation pooling in my hands. He must've had this drink for a while.

"Sorry, have fun." I say.

Chapter Nine

I turn and head off towards Joey. I don't get any greeting from his friends as I approach. If this were a party full of my own guests, I probably wouldn't make it ten steps without someone stopping me. I don't think anyone here knows who I am. I've never been close with Joey's friends and have been kept separate from his work life for as long as I've known him. When my eyes meet his, he is stuck on me. It feels welcoming. It makes my feet move towards him without control. I walk up and wrap my arms around his torso, with my chin on his chest, staring straight up. It feels nice.

"I want you to meet my colleagues," he says turning over to face the group of people surrounding him.

We're holding hands and he's smiling. He seems really happy, unlike how he was before the party. It's crazy how quickly his fire can be put out… And how quickly it can be lit back up again.

He goes through the line, introducing other surgeons, his bosses, and a few nurses. He stops on the nurse standing to his left, Dana. He talks about her for what feels like five minutes. He goes on about how much promise he can see in her and how he thinks she'll go far. He says that he could see her becoming a doctor someday long after he's transferred. I guess he's already told everyone that he's moving. I've never heard him speak so highly of someone, especially someone with only four months experience on the job.

I smile at everyone, introduce myself and then I fade into the background. A man introduced as Dr. Scott David takes over the conversation. I'm not paying attention to his words. I just watch the lines of his mouth open and close again until it's the next guys turn to speak. The conversation is stale, yet everyone seems to be enjoying it. Everyone except for me. I tap Joey on the shoulder and excuse myself to check on dinner.

I walk into the kitchen and take a breath. For as large as our home is, our kitchen is small. There are about fifteen people moving around and there's really no place for me.

I ask the head server about how the food is coming along. She tells me that it'll all be ready to go in ten minutes. Just on time; Joey will be pleased. We're setting up stations throughout the room with different styles of food. Our guests can head out to each booth and grab a little bit of whatever they're craving. This is a new trend in this month's Lifestyle411: my only insight into the party planning business besides the internet. I always grab a copy each month and keep it in my purse. Pathetic, I know. I don't have the courage to ask Joey if I can take some time off to do night classes. I know he'd never approve. Throwing his parties is a lot of work; I hardly have space to breathe during the months surrounding each event.

I give the go-ahead to bring the food out as soon as it's ready, then I leave the kitchen to take a lap of the house and show my face. It's the time of night where everyone is at least four or five drinks in and feeling tipsy. This means that if I'm stopped, I'll surely be trapped in a conversation for ten minutes or more. I immediately get pulled to the side by Joey's sisters, Tab and Lydia who are visiting from the States. They're both older than him and overly protective. There isn't a thing that I could do right by them. Anything Joey does, they agree with. It's toxic and gross considering he does a lot of things that I don't approve of.

"Hey, sis," Lydia says pulling me in as I walk by.

"Hey ladies, are you enjoying the party?" I ask.

I'm letting the snarky comments slide. I know that Lydia doesn't consider me to be her sister and I stopped trying to gain her approval a long time ago.

"It's nice. A bit much though, don't you think?" she asks me, as if she doesn't know that I planned the entire thing myself.

"Yeah, I guess," I answer.

"Where's the birthday boy anyways?" Tab asks. She doesn't completely hate me, she just tends to be two-faced: siding with her brother and sister as soon as tension heats up between us. "We want to give him his gift. We pitched in with mom and dad this year. Since my divorce, and Lydia finally having the baby, we're short on money," she adds.

I forgot that Lydia had her baby. She hasn't brought him by at all. She didn't want me coming to the hospital to visit either. I've only seen pictures from Joey's phone. She's lost all of her baby weight easily because she's a personal trainer and you could hardly tell she was even pregnant at all. For most of her pregnancy she looked like she was only five months along, even at the end.

"He's over by the food, making sure his work friends eat enough. I'm sure he'll love whatever it is you guys got him," I try to fluff up the conversation. "I'm glad you both made it tonight. I know it's probably been difficult with the divorce, I'm so sorry Tab," I say, touching her shoulder. I choose to disregard Lydia.

"Oh, I'm fine. It took me two weeks to shake off that piece of garbage. I'm sure you saw it coming. I'm just glad I don't have to drive up with him yapping in the passenger seat on the way to Christmas dinners anymore," she laughs.

I see one of the workers waving me down and I take that as my cue to leave. When everyone is drinking, you have to take every escape you can.

"It was so nice catching up but I think a waiter is calling me over. Just let me know if you need anything else, I'll be around somewhere," I say, walking off.

The waiter tells me that they ran out of scotch and asks if I want someone to go get more. The only two people that I know who drink scotch are Joey and Fallon. I nod, signalling him to send someone to the liquor store. I start making my way over to the bar where I see Alex and her entire wedding party raising their arms to toast a shot. As I approach them, they make room for me to join in. Alex orders another round and the bartender looks over at me as if she's seeking my approval. I nod with a smile and wonder how many shots they've all taken.

Fallon is attentive and participating in the group's discussion. He's a completely different man than I saw sulking at the bar an hour ago. His arm is slung around Alex's sister, Jessica. I'm not too shocked by this; he has a thing for short blonde girls. Plus, I can tell that he's doing this just to get a rise out of me. It's hardly convincing because he's staring at me the same way he was at Alex's party and I doubt he'll make it through the night without getting the twins mixed up. Those girls are so high maintenance, I feel bad for any man who takes on the challenge of dating one of them. I sip my drink, trying not to smile but I end up laughing and my drink bubbles up in my cup.

I have to admit that it's hard seeing him with someone else, even if it's just to get me worked up. Fallon turns to face the bar, grabbing a tray of shots and circling it back around to the group. We all take a blue and green coloured shot from the tray and lift it in the air. Fallon begins to speak; I assume he's going to make the toast.

"I know that this is a party for, Joey," he says pausing. "But I want to make a toast as best man, to my best friend, Daniel, and his beautiful wife-to-be, Alexandra. I have known these two for almost six years as a couple and I knew that we would eventually be here today, toasting to their marriage. You only find a love like this once, right Josephine?" Everyone stops and stares at me in confusion. My mouth falls open and we all stand silent for a moment before Fallon continues, "Cheers to a life of loyalty, love, passion, and happiness," he says shooting his drink into his mouth.

I'm now overanalyzing all of his words. The only thing I can think to do to draw attention away from it is make a speech of my own. I feel like Fallon's not in his right mind to be making speeches like this. Besides, my husband's birthday party is not where I want what happened between us to come out.

"I would also like to say a few words…" I say, I have no idea where this is going but I start speaking anyways.

"Thank you all for coming today. This is just a taste of the partying that we're going to be doing in a few months. Fallon and I have come up with an amazing bachelor party idea."

As I say this, Fallon and I are locking eyes. This time though, my mind falls to what Alex told me earlier about Fallon's parents. I feel a drastic change in my expression; a bright smile turning into a look of disgust. I feel sick to my stomach. His face drops too. I think he knows that she told me somehow. He turns to leave the circle.

"Um, there's an email I will send you all about it this week. Cheers to Alex and Dan," I quickly blurt out before turning to walk in the opposite direction.

None of what I said makes any sense. I feel so horrible. The last thing I wanted to do tonight was make him think about his parents. Luckily, I see Jessica follow him. Hopefully she can distract him for a while.

I need some air. I'm cutting straight across the party, trying to get to the back door as fast as possible. I think I hear people calling me. I can't stop, though; I need to be outside for a second. I open my back-patio doors and step outside. There are even more people out here. The pot lights are on, lighting up an empty pathway along the wrap-around deck attached to my home. I walk slowly to the front of the house, grabbing a full bottle of beer off the ledge of the deck and taking a swig. I don't care that I don't know who it belongs to at this point.

The clicking of my heels along the wooden slats is comforting: the sound is pulling me back to sanity. I haven't experienced anxiety this severely before tonight. Not in a way where the walls feel like they're closing in on me.

As I approach the front of my house I look out and see the side door to the garage open. Joey was out here hours ago. He must have started drinking early on and forgot to close it. He doesn't normally forget these kinds of things. I walk up to the door and step through it, softly pulling it behind me. It's pitch black in here, besides the light of Joey's new car. The side door of the car is fully open, and the inside light is on. I'm confused but I continue in towards the car. I see movement and I begin think someone's out here. Did someone take the keys to his car? At a party this big anyone could have just grabbed them off the hook. I take cautious steps, feeling unsteady. As I stand at the back of his car, I start to hear moans. Familiar moans. Joey's moans. I reach my hand back in shock trying to grab onto something for balance. I take hold of the tool rack that is behind me. I look down at the floor and see his pants sitting around his ankles. Son of a bitch.

Joey has his leg propped up on the floor of the car while the rest of his body remains outside of it, and whoever he's with is lying across the backseat. I see him reach down and pull the leg of a woman over his shoulder. He then uses his other hand to grab her hips and pull her further into him.

"You're so sexy," he breathes out.

I feel like I'm going to be sick for the second time tonight. He has no idea that I'm standing right here. Something in me is holding me back from grabbing him and pulling him off of her. It's probably the fact that I know he could hurt me way worse than I could ever hurt him. Or maybe it's the fact that I was with Fallon in our bed only a few months ago. I'm unsure. As much as I don't want to go back inside, I surely don't want to be out here. I turn away from them, listening to the buckle of Joey's pants rattling along the floor underneath him as I walk out. I turn to close the side door and it seems to be jammed open. His tie is stuck underneath it. I yank it out, hearing the door slam behind me. I don't wait to see if he comes out. I walk back around the house and shove the tie in the pocket of my dress.

I slide back into the empty booth that Alex and I were talking in earlier. I scroll my finger along the bottles of alcohol displayed on the table and take my pick: tequila. I normally despise the drink but tonight, there's something I despise more. If Joey wanted to, he could leave me, and he knows this. He knows that this relationship runs on his time. I have to tag along until he decides that we're done. I don't want to know what would happen if I tried leaving. I sip from the bottle and Alex slides into the booth beside me.

"I shouldn't have told you all that earlier," she says apologetically.

"It's okay, I'm glad I know," I reply. "It's just hard seeing him hurt like this."

"I know. He's off with Jess now. I saw them head out not too long ago. I think he'll be okay. He just needs a few bottles of water and a Tylenol," she says.

She then starts talking about the bachelor and bachelorette parties. She says that she's always wanted to visit a place like Piper's Peak and that she's glad Dan and the guys will be there with us.

Across the room I see Joey walk into the house. He looks around and reaches down, zipping up his fly. What a gentleman. I breathe in heavily and look up. When my head comes back down, I see Dana follow him inside. I should have known she's the girl he was with. He doesn't think she's talented at all, he only sees her cleavage and Bambi eyes.

I turn back to Alex and she's still going on about all the planning we'll need to do. I stare at her, not really listening, but trying to mirror the facial expressions she's showing me. It's not long before Dan and Joey slide into the booth with us. Joey immediately starts his search. I know that he has no idea who closed the side door of the garage. He just wants to make sure it wasn't me.

"How about a drink for the husbands," Joey suggests. He grabs the other two bottles of liquor from the table and passes them to Alex and Dan. "We should be taking a page from Josephine's book."

A smug smile crosses his face. He's sitting across from me, and Dan across from Alex.

"Thanks, babe," I say, giving the biggest fake smile I own.

I can tell that he bought it because I see his guard go down.

"Are you ladies enjoying the party?" he asks.

"Yes, it's been awesome. Thanks again, for inviting my friends," Alex responds.

"Yeah, it's been great so far!" I say overenthusiastically. "Oh, by the way, I was walking through the garage and found one of your ties. This one's your favourite, I wouldn't want you to lose it," I say tossing it to him over the table.

Joey catches the tie and I see his face drop. I smile, triumphant.

Chapter Ten

four months until the wedding...

Joey hasn't brought up the fact that we both know he cheated on me and having this kind of information sitting inside of me with nowhere to fall is unsettling. You would think that he'd be trying to rebuild what he broke but unfortunately, he's been worse than ever. He's acting as if he's angry with me for catching him being unfaithful, and his silence is my punishment. Last week, he was brushing his teeth while I was in the shower and through the reflection of the mirror I saw marks all over his chest. As soon as he left, I cried uncontrollably. I know I'm no better; that's the main reason I've remained silent.

I don't know how much longer I can go without addressing the issue. I'm staring at Joey's sideways face as he eats an apple and flips through a pile of files with his other hand. I watch him intently, missing the man that my husband used to be. I wonder if he's still in there somewhere.

Joey usually follows a strict routine. He wakes up and showers, puts on his work clothes, eats breakfast, takes a mug of black coffee, and leaves the house, not returning home until after sundown. However, since he found out I knew about his affair, he eats breakfast in his night clothes and showers every other day. Normally a change in seasons causes his emotions to stir. When snow coats the ground and the Christmas lights go up, he becomes more cheerful. For some reason this year he's remained stone cold. It's the middle of January, the lights have already come down and the holidays are long gone, yet he still hasn't made his shift.

We're falling apart even more than usual and the worst part is, I'm scared to ask him about it. The only bright side to his absence is that Joey doesn't seem to care as much about what I do. I've been using the extra time to see my therapist. I have an appointment with her at 1:30p.m. today. I tell Joey that I'm going to see my mom for the afternoon. She *did* invite me over, but I declined. It's a semi truthful lie.

Half of the trip to meet Faye is spent trying to keep my eyes focused on the road. They blur in and out of reality the further I drive and the snow isn't helping. When I arrive, I step out of my car and walk into the building. The inside is plain and depressing; the hallways are lined with couples who seem to be undergoing marriage counselling, and teenagers with notepads and tissue boxes. Joey told me once that he thinks counselling is absolutely pathetic. I think he'd benefit from it whether he'd admit it or not.

I'm always relieved when I'm about to see Faye; she's the only person in my life that I'm completely honest with. I'm sitting on a chair just outside of her office, staring down at my black heels. I begin knocking the snow off the bottom of my shoe against the chair. This is the first time I've dressed up since the party. Thinking back to everything that unfolded that night, I realize she has no clue what she's in for during this session.

She pops her head out of the door and calls me in. I walk into her office and sit down across from her, letting out a heavy sigh as I meet the chair. It feels like her office is the only place I can actually breathe.

"Thank you for seeing me," I say as she greets me.

"You know my doors are always open for you, Josie," she replies. "This is the first time in a while that we've had an in-person meeting, though," she analyzes.

"I know," I say smiling softly. It feels so stupid that I'm this excited to see her. She only likes me because I pay her to but it's better company than Joey, who hates me for free.

"Well, as you know, I threw a birthday party for Joey a few months ago... A lot happened that night."

"Yes, you were working on this one for a long time. Did he like the car?" she asks.

"I can't tell; he's hardly spoken two words to me since that night," I say. I immediately begin laughing and realize I must seem crazy to her.

"What's so funny?" she asks.

"I actually know the answer to your question... Yes, he loved that car. I caught him fucking a nurse from his hospital in the backseat of it," I say.

"Oh, god. I'm so sorry," she says putting her hand over her mouth.

"Well, *I'm* not surprised. I mean, what right do I have to be upset, I'm no better," I look down. She already knows what transpired with Fallon after Alex's engagement party.

"The relationship between you and Fallon isn't exactly the same. You've known Fallon for years. You told me you had genuine feelings for him. How do you feel about him now?" she asks.

"I feel a lot of different things for Fallon, it's hard to explain. I'm trying not to think too much about him right now," I pause and continue, "I know that Joey doesn't have a clue about what happened with Fallon. I just don't understand why he won't talk to me."

"Do you think he's freezing you out because he was caught?" she asks in reply.

"I think you're spot on," I say, my fingers tracing the back of my neck where Joey grabbed me. "I told you about what happened when he grabbed my wrist… well he did something similar at the party. He was holding the back of my neck so tight, it scared me. I don't even want to think of what he would do if I started a conversation about catching him cheating," I say. My eyes are now watering.

"Confronting someone like him might not be the best thing to do," she says. "Have you considered leaving him?"

"Yes, so many times, but I know I can't. He's all that I have and I'm scared to start over," I say.

"If you're not willing or able to leave him on your own then what I suggest you do is talk to someone in your life about it. Two people are more powerful than one. If you open up to someone else that can help, you might have more motivation to leave," she says. "And if you can't do that, then you need to get him help. If he can't see the problem, he'll never change."

The worst part of it all has been holding in my emotions. I feel like they've all built up for so long that they're beginning to boil over. I'm scared that they'll release at the wrong time.

"That's not the only thing that happened at the party," I say, trying to pull the conversation in another direction. She raises her eyebrows as a sign for me to continue.

"Fallon was there. I guess Joey invited Alex and the entire wedding party," I add.

"How was that?" she asks.

"Not good. Alex told me how Fallon's parents died. It's actually pretty horrible… They were murdered. And I guess that he was there when it all happened. He heard the entire thing and was so drunk and scared that he couldn't bring himself to move. Fallon found out that he was the one who left the security gate open and that's how the man got into their house," I say. Suddenly I'm crying again.

I can tell she's shocked further. She has the same look on her face that I did when Alex told me.

"I tried not to bring it up, but Fallon had Alex's sister wrapped under his arm and he kept alluding to the fact that we slept together," I say knowing I completely overanalyzed the situation. "I just needed to stop him from talking and my emotions got the best of me. I didn't say anything, but I think he could read it in my eyes. He left the party right after that."

"Wow, that's a lot. Are you guys still having your coffee meetings? Maybe you could call him and meet for lunch to talk about what happened," she suggests. "He's been through a lot and so have you. It seems like you both could use a friend right now."

"We have been meeting but not since after the party; he's been away on vacation. Besides, he was so drunk at my party I don't even think he remembers. He's already suspicious of Joey. He can't stand him. If I'm going to tell someone, I'm going to tell someone impartial," I say.

"The only impartial people are the ones who are restricted under doctor-patient confidentiality," she says with concern. "You should call him."

Before I know it, it's been an hour and our meeting ends. I gather my things and walk back down that sad hallway and to my car. When I get to my car I sit inside of it, start it, and wait for it to heat up. I feel the cold winter air creep through the window, it feels nice against my flushed cheeks. I reach into my glove box to grab the unopened pack of cigarettes and lighter that I've kept there since meeting Joey. I'm not sure if they've gone stale or not. I just keep them unless I get too stressed to cope. I've never smoked before, but I figured that it's better to have them accessible rather than trying something crazy in the heat of the moment. I rip open the packaging, flip the lid, and then pull out my phone. I scroll through my contacts until I reach Jennifer. My finger hovers above the dial button for a few beats before I hit call.

Each time it rings, my chest tightens. I begin trying to light a cigarette when Fallon's voice greets me.

"Josie, is everything okay?" he asks. It seems like it's been forever since I heard his voice.

"Hi, Fallon. Yeah, everything's fine," I reply, flicking my lighter, trying to get the damn thing to start.

"Are you smoking a cigarette?" he asks laughing. "We both know you don't smoke. Plus, you need to inhale if you want it to light."

"Yes, actually, I am," I say proudly. I don't want him to think he knows everything about me.

"Let me know if you need help," he pauses waiting for me to figure it out. Once he stops hearing the flick of the lighter, he continues, "I'm glad you called. Your party was a lot of fun, thanks again for having me," he says. I guess he doesn't remember what happened.

"I'm glad you came… I am not sure if you remember, but you left early, during my toast to Alex and Dan. I just wanted to check in on you, since you haven't texted or called. I was wondering if we were meeting soon to work on the wedding stuff," I ramble.

"Oh, I had a lot to drink that night. Don't worry, it wasn't anything you did. I was just tired," he says coolly. "I've been pretty busy these past few weeks, but I've actually been meaning to call you."

It feels like he's saying this as a way to make me feel better.

"It's okay, Fallon. You don't need to see me if you don-"
I start to say before he stops me.

"Josephine, Josephine, Josephine, do you not remember
what I told you? I would see you every day if I could. We
both know that," he says. He's so bold; taking what he
wants.

"Oh," I laugh in surprise. "So, when do you want to
meet then? I have a lot of new ideas. The bachelor
parties are only three months away."

"I want to meet you next Saturday at Merl's. It's on the
corner of Brant and Rochester, downtown. How does
10:00p.m. sound?" he asks. Maybe he *has* been planning
to see me.

"That should work; my schedule's been pretty open
lately. It's sort of late though, and I don't figure we'll get
a lot of work done at one of the busiest sports bars in the
city," I reply.

"Don't worry about that; I just want to see you. I'll text
you if the details change. Otherwise, I'll see you then,"
he says, hanging up his phone.

I sit back in my seat, thanking Faye in my mind. I
wonder if he would have made those plans if I hadn't
called him.

--

When I walk into the house it looks untouched. Joey must be spending the night away again. I take off my shoes and hang up my purse. I slip off my dress and toss it down the loop of stairs leading to the basement. I stand in my bra and underwear and start walking upstairs to grab a shower when I hear movement. I guess he's home after all. As I make it halfway up, Joey blocks the top entryway of the staircase. The soft carpet underneath my feet becomes cool and my hand grabs the wooden railing. Half of me feels like running back down the stairs. I can't read him right now.

"Come here," he says sternly.

My mind is screaming, *"don't do it,"* but my body complies with him and I move lifelessly to the top. I approach him and we stand face to face. His eyes are blank and he breathes heavily. The smell of scotch clouds over me, burning my nose. I can feel that he's not happy.

"Do you want to tell me why you didn't visit your poor mother today?" he asks, enunciating every word that comes from his mouth. "She must be worried sick."

"I can explain that, Joey," I say. My heart is pounding and my head is dizzy.

He lets out a loud and obnoxious laugh that sits right in front of my face. I'm afraid to pull back.

"No need to explain, I already called her. I let her know that you've been acting out of control these past few months. I told her all about the outbursts you've been having and she agrees that you need to get some help. She was so worried about you that she offered to drive over, but I told her not to. I told her I'd call the therapists offered through my work to make sure you get your feelings out," he says through his teeth. "So, you tell me Josephine, where the fuck were you?"

I feel him all over my body and he hasn't even touched me.

"I was with Jennifer," I lie. "She's going through a lot and needed someone to talk to. I didn't want to embarrass her by telling you." I'm unsure if he buys it.

He grabs my finger, the one where my wedding ring sits and slides it off. He then presses it into my neck. Deeper and deeper until I squeal.

"Please stop, Joey. I'm not lying!" I shout, trying not to cry.

"Well, you tell your friend Jennifer that she's not the only one going through personal issues. I have a wife who's a lying bitch," he scoffs.

He pulls the ring that's now damp with blood from my neck and throws it. He then grabs my shoulders and pushes me down the first set of stairs and onto the landing. It's only five steps down, but my head thumps off of the wall. *I'm still awake. I'm okay. I'm alive.* I repeat these three thoughts over in my head.

Joey walks past my body and down into the kitchen. He grabs the orange juice from the fridge and pours himself a glass.

"Are you okay?" he asks calmly, as if the last five minutes didn't just happen.

I've pulled myself up onto the wall. The only thing that's bleeding is my neck and forearm which must have scraped against a loose nail. I nod in his direction and see that he's looking me dead in my eyes.

"Good. Now, I've left the number for Dr. Christianson on the counter. I'm going to call him to see if he can have a session with you over the phone. When I spoke with him earlier, he said as long as we call before eight that he should be able to speak with you today. You might want to go up and take a quick shower as it will likely be a video call. You can thank me later," he says as he walks over to the table to pick up his cellphone.

I walk upstairs, my ankle is sore from the fall. I'm trying to think of what I did to make him so fucking angry, but I draw a blank. I can't believe he lied to my mom. I don't speak with her often enough for her to know who to believe. I turn on the faucet to insinuate that I'm having a shower. I lean over the sink and sip water in my hands. I then grab a cloth and dab at the mark on my neck and arm. They're both dried out now. I grab my foundation and press onto it. This cannot be good for an open wound but I'm sure that's the least of Joey's concerns. I have twenty minutes before my fake call with Joey's therapist friend. I want to scream. I sink my body into the corner between the shower and the wall, letting out soft sobs into my shirt.

I can't remember when things became so bad between Joey and I. He's always been opinionated and a bit cold, but nothing like this. We've been together for four years and he's never done what he did to me tonight. He's gotten into altercations with more than just friends of mine; he's gotten into them with my family too. All except for my mom. He's somehow been able to convince her that he's a saint. I sit and think about all the people I've lost in my life because of him. My college friends all stopped inviting me places; Alex and Dan stopped having me over and even my own family has cut me out for the most part.

I think back to two years ago when we hosted Easter at our house. We hadn't hosted any holidays since we had been married and I was so excited. Holidays for my family were huge. I'm sure they still are; I wouldn't know since I'm no longer invited to them.

It was time to sit and cut the turkey. I was in the kitchen chatting with my mom and pouring wine. This was back when my parents were still married, and I think my dad cutting me off had something to do with their divorce. Joey yelled out for us to come sit but we didn't hear him because we were speaking too loudly. We were both a bit tipsy since we'd each consumed an entire bottle of wine without realizing it. We'd started by drinking mimosas in the morning and didn't stop drinking until the food was brought out to eat. On my way out of the kitchen I was carrying the stuffing that Joey's mom had sent over the evening before, and I snagged my toe on the carpet underneath the dining room table. I dropped the entire plate onto the floor. Joey stood up so quickly that his chair fell over and he started screaming at me that I was no longer allowed to drink at family events. My dad quickly stood up in my defence and Joey didn't take it too well. They started yelling at each other until Joey tried to hit my dad and missed. This was only the second time in our relationship where he showed his true colours to me. It was hard not to defend Joey when I only saw this side of him once every few years. Besides, he was my husband and I was raised to stick by my partner no matter what. Those were our wedding vows, right?

They didn't end up hitting each other, but they did take things outside and onto our front lawn. My dad was so upset that he just left without saying a word. After my dad left, my older brother Nate had to hold my younger brother Cam, back from attacking Joey. Nate and Cam then decided that it would probably be for the best if they just left, leaving my mother, Joey and I to eat an entire turkey dinner by ourselves. Joey and my mom turned the evening into a gabfest about my dad.

It was horrible. I haven't spoken to my father since then; Joey doesn't allow it. Every time the holidays come around, he books us tickets to go and visit his family out of the country. It makes sense to me now that what I have with Joey is toxic. However, it's too late to change anything. It's too late to make things right with the people I no longer speak to because of him. They've already tried, and I shut them all down.

I stand up and begin to wash my face. I change into sweatpants, a loose t-shirt and a cardigan, tying my hair up into a bun. I slide my reading glasses over my nose and head downstairs. I quickly realize that Joey will be watching my staged therapy session as he's propped on a bar stool picking up where he left off with his papers from this morning. I sit in my reading chair and hug my knees into my chest. I'm waiting for the doctor to call me and trying to think of what I am going to say when he inevitably asks the question, "what made you decide to start therapy?"

Maybe I can talk about all of the relationships in my life that have ended by Joey's wrongdoing. I can try and find a way to say how I'm feeling in the hopes that Dr. Christianson understands that Joey's the problem without the accusations directly leaving my mouth. It's now 7:00p.m. on the nose and Dr. Christianson is calling me.

"Hey there, Josephine, it's very nice to meet you," he says cheerfully.

"Hi Dr. Christianson, thank you for speaking with me on such short notice," I quickly reply, insinuating that this was a last-minute arrangement.

I see Joey's eyes shift to me, warning me to watch myself.

"Not a problem. We only have twenty minutes today as I have another appointment in the next hour. I just wanted to meet, do some quick introductions, and go over some temporary coping strategies to tide you over until we can have a deeper conversation. How does that sound?"

"Good," I say.

"Great. So, tell me a bit about yourself and what brings you to me today," he says.

Perfect. The first question is the one I knew he would ask me. The one I was dreading. I tell him exactly what I was thinking earlier. I tell him I'm a housewife who is experiencing loneliness. I tell him that Joey is the only person I have in my life who understands me and that my family has alienated themselves from me since Joey and I were married. I lie to him, but I feel like I've put enough truth in there for him to read between the lines.

"I see. Well, that's very insightful and helpful to my understanding," he says. He then goes on a ten-minute rant about what I could do to help myself until we speak again. He doesn't seem to understand what I'm trying to say. He says that from what I've told him, he thinks we need to work on putting down my walls in order to let people in. After he says this, I tune him out for the rest of the session; he's just Joey's puppet and I can't stand to listen any longer.

Chapter Eleven

I open my eyes for the first time today and they feel heavy. Floods of what happened last night invade my mind. I don't remember what happened after my phone call with Dr. Christianson. I hope that doesn't mean I have a concussion. I probably should have gone to see the doctor before letting myself fall asleep. I heard that it's very dangerous to sleep with a head injury. My arm is aching for some reason. I look down and see the cut along my forearm. My head must have been hurting so badly that I didn't even notice how bad it had gotten. It's nothing crazy, but it's sore. It's likely infected from trying to cover it up with foundation.

I see Joey standing in the doorway. I don't know how long he's been there. He walks over to the edge of the bed and sits beside me. He's sitting on the unmade and wrinkled portion of the bed, which tells me he slept beside me last night. He takes his hand and strokes my head, feeling the goose egg on its side. I wince. I don't ask him to stop touching me, though. I will take any affection I can get from him at this point. I never know how long his sincerity will last. I'm not sure if he's trying to give me a silent apology or not. I can't tell if he has any humanity left in him or if he's blocked what happened from his mind. After a few moments of silence, he begins to speak.

"Your mom is here; she brought breakfast. You should come down and see her. We can take a look at that cut once she leaves," he says laying the cardigan I wore last night beside me and standing up to go downstairs.

He seems happy today, but I know this is just a façade to entertain my mother. He told me last night that they spoke and I can't even begin to think of what their conversation consisted of. I stand up, put the cardigan on, and slide my slippers over my feet before heading downstairs. As I walk towards the railing, I can hear a conversation between the two. Although it's a long way down, there are hardly any walls on the first floor, leading conversations to shoot straight up the staircase.

"How did she seem after we spoke?" I hear my mom whisper.

"Not good, if I'm being honest, April," Joey says releasing a sigh after his words.

"I bet it's all of this distance from her father and the boys. She never talks to me about them. I don't

understand why he doesn't just call her. The man is sixty
years old. So what? A little fight happens and that's it?
That's not what family does. I told him how wonderful
you are to our girl," she replies.

"I know. I'm so grateful she has you. Your opinion
means everything to her," he says as I enter the room.

"Sweetheart!" my mom says running over to me.

I stand a half a foot above her and she still holds me as if
I were able to fit in her arms. I begin to cry, and I can see
a stream of my tears piling onto her shirt. I look at Joey
in the background, unpacking the things she brought for
us. He gives me a compassionate look that feels
disingenuous.

"Sit honey, let's talk," she suggests. I know that this can't
be good.

"You didn't have to come all the way up, mom. If I'm
being honest, I don't even know why you're here," I say
flatly. My mom and I don't see each other often. Her
and Joey have similar personalities, so I keep our
relationship at a distance. We have developed a strong
friendship over the years, but it's primarily through the
telephone.

"Joey called me yesterday afternoon. He said he didn't
know where you were and was worried. It was so kind of
him to include me in this and for him to open up about
what's been going on," she says. *What is she talking about?*

"Yes," Joey starts. "You've been acting irrational lately, Josie."

"Joey thought it would be best if I came over to check on you. I think that starting therapy is very noble of you," she says placing her hand on top of mine.

This is why I haven't told anyone in my life aside from Alex that I am seeing a therapist. They say things like, "you're so brave," and "how noble of you," like I am some kind of psychopath.

"You're hardly home anymore; you've been drinking constantly. You're hanging out with all the wrong people... we're worried," he says softly. He stands behind me and wraps his arms around my shoulders.

"Yes, you've already said that," I sigh, instantly regretting it.

"Maybe you should come stay with me for a while," my mom suggests, drawing Joey's attention directly to her and completely distracting him from what I just said. I breathe deeply in relief.

I know that she should be concerned, but there's much more going on here than the lies Joey's been feeding her. It's breaking me inside. I want to go with her, but Joey would never allow that. At this point, I don't even know if she would believe me if I were to open up to her. She thinks too highly of Joey.

"Mom, it's fine. I think Dr. Christianson is going to help a lot," I say to ease her mind. Meanwhile, mine is scattered all over the place.

My words seem to settle her and we sit to eat breakfast. My mom has brought pastries, bagels, a fruit tray, all the spreads you could imagine, and more. She's yet again being over the top. Breakfast conversation is led by her; I hardly say a word. She does a back and forth with Joey about coping mechanisms for anxiety and depression that she read online. Joey gets up and brings a notepad to the table. He begins to jot down her suggestions. She starts talking about symptoms of bipolar disorder, insinuating that I may have it.

I start pondering the thought that they might actually be right. What if this *is* just all in my head? Maybe there *is* something wrong with me? My eyes start swelling again.

"Oh, dear," my mom says. "You see, Joey? All of this emotion cannot be normal." She dabs a cloth over my eyes.

I feel useless and helpless. Most of all, I feel confused.

"Thank you, for this wonderful breakfast, April," Joey says. He wipes his mouth and pushes his chair out, kissing my mother on the head and then kissing me on the cheek. "I know it was a long drive and we thank you so much for coming. I'll walk you out. I need to get going too," he adds.

I don't understand why he's asking her to leave so soon.

"Oh no, thank *you*, son. That would be great, you're such a gentleman," she replies, winking at me.

She gives me another hug and tells me she'll call me tomorrow morning to check back on me. As she pulls away, I feel my last shred of hope leave with her. It makes my chest burn. As the door closes behind them, I understand why Joey does this; he's trying to show me that he controls me in absolutely every way. He controls when I see my friends, when I see my mom, and when it all ends. Leaving me alone, horrifically alone.

Their chatter runs all the way down the driveway. It stops as I hear their cars start. I listen as the noise from their engine's fade along with them. I start wondering if Joey is right about me. I need clarity, but I don't trust anyone to help me with this right now. I would vent to Alex if we weren't in the middle of planning her wedding. I make a promise to myself to tell her as soon as she comes back from her honeymoon. For now, I have to keep what's going on to myself.

--

I decide to go for a run. This is one of the activities given to me by Dr. Christianson. Joey told me he would be watching our security cameras today to see if I follow his orders. Things are going to be fine; I think to myself. Joey is leaving this week for a business trip, to some conference in Florida. He'll be gone for two weeks and I tell myself that I can manage until then. I feel a bit sad letting my happiness depend on Joey's travel schedule, but it will have to do for right now.

Since it's a cold day I put on leggings and sweater to prepare for the crisp and windy air. It looks like it's either going to snow or it already has. I put my headphones in and blast some alternative music; nothing too heavy because I need this time to think. I walk out the front door, following the same path Joey and my mom took. I begin by jogging. The cold wind feels so good on my eyes and face.

The only thing that this run is making me feel is angry. Angry that we live in a suburban neighbourhood full of rich happy families: babies in strollers, couples holding hands, elderly people with their grandchildren, and all the rest of that bullshit. I realize that I look into the same houses every day and know nothing about the people inside. Joey and I live our life together openly. We're a book for the world to read. We don't have blinds on the windows of our open concept home; our house is transparent. Four floors of complete exposure, yet somehow nobody sees the bruises all over my body. Not once has anyone reported an argument. It's possible that they recognize him as one of the lead cardiac surgeons in our country. Or maybe, they just don't care.

I shake my head; I don't want to cry again. I'm all the way by the pond now, watching as the birds glide across the sky and swoop down into the pond. They drag their bodies in the water as they land. This winter it hasn't become cold enough for the water to freeze over. The birds still linger around as if they don't know whether or not to leave. They remind me of myself.

My anger begins to dissolve as my mind drifts from Joey. I'm not an angry person by nature and I hate that Joey has made me become one. When I'm not in our house I'm able to think clearly. I know that I'm not the problem. I'm almost certain of that now. His games may work on my mother, but I won't let them work on me. I tell myself that I'm strong, though the aches in my ankle and forearm tell me otherwise. I doubt that running is really good for me right now, but it's better than the repercussions of defying Joey.

I pick back up in my run as the wind rolls beneath me, across the snow and into the water. It makes me think of my time with Alex, before Joey. One night in particular: when we convinced twin brothers that we were sisters. The four of us spent the night walking all the way across town to go to a club. It took us three hours to get there, but we didn't have enough money for a cab both ways. It's funny how now I could take a cab across the country and Joey probably wouldn't even notice the dent in his bank account. I was much happier when I didn't have money. I wish I could tell myself to hold out for a man who could provide more than just financial security.

I pull out my phone and call Alex. It's only four months until her wedding. We still have so much to do.

"Josie, how's it going babe?" she asks.

"I'm good. It's nice to hear your voice," I say.

"Is everything okay?" she replies.

"Yeah. I'm good, just out of breath. I'm out for a run and just remembered that we need to go pick out your cake," I say making something up.

"Oh, I must have forgotten to tell you; we already got one," she says.

"No, you're right. You did say something about it," I say, unsure if she's told me this or not.

"While I have you on the phone, a little birdie told me that you're going out with Fallon this weekend. Is that true?" she asks, laughing.

"Oh my god, why would he even tell you that?" I question. She makes such a big deal out of everything. "We're just meeting to do some last-minute planning," I add.

"To pick out a wedding cake that I already ordered?" she slickly fires back.

"Yeah, exactly," I answer.

"You better call me and tell me everything," she says. "Maybe I can come over beforehand and we can pick out an outfit?"

"Alex, this isn't a date. But yeah, you can come over. It'll be nice to see you. I haven't seen you since the party, and Joey will be out of town," I say. I feel horrible that I only invite her over when he's away.

"Sounds great. Anyways, I've got to go; we have Dan's friend over. And not Fallon in case you were wondering," she laughs.

"Talk soon," I say, hanging up the phone.

I put my phone away and continue where I left off. This run is going well. My ankle is swelling up the more that I put pressure on it, but I'll just take an ibuprofen and lay some ice on it when I get home. I pick up my pace to end off my run. I end up doing three kilometers; I'm impressed considering I haven't run in years.

I decide to grab a coffee and walk back home. I walk across the street along the side of my favourite cafe; the one I always go to, where they know my order. I peer in through the glass window, looking at the table where Fallon and I once sat. I blink hard for a moment; I see Joey sitting inside with a woman that I don't recognize. He begins to smile, and I watch as his smile turns into a laugh.

He has what looks like a large coffee in a glass cup made with milk. With goddam milk. I turn around and step away from the window, deflating a little more. I don't cry or yell. I don't feel anything. What's the point? This has become a disturbing routine for us. I catch him with a woman, and I never confront him about it. I walk back across the street and it begins to snow lightly, emulating how I feel inside because I no longer have the emotion in me to show it on the outside. I watch as Joey and the woman stand up and walk towards the door. He opens it for her and she steps out into the cold. He then takes his jacket off and wraps it around her as they turn to walk in the opposite direction.

I decide that I've seen enough. I begin walking back home and see Joey's car parked along the side street. I can tell he's trying to be somewhat discreet, but I don't see the point in that anymore. It just shows how little he knows about me to be having an affair in a coffee shop that I visit almost every morning.

Chapter Twelve

"I brought you a present," Alex says as she walks around the corner holding a bag with a ribbon hanging off of it. "I know your birthday isn't until tomorrow, but I figured you're my best friend and my maid of honour, so you deserve to be spoiled."

"Thank you," I gasp, giving her a hug. "And thanks for coming to help me. God knows I could use it. I just want to fit in. I doubt I have anything to wear; I only have suits and blouses. People are going to think I'm a grandmother."

"Open the bag, maybe you'll find some inspiration in there," she says raising her eyebrows.

"You did not!" I shriek. I lift a red dress out of the bag. It looks brand new but isn't; in fact, I had completely forgotten about it. It's the dress I wore the night that I met Fallon. "That's so sweet, but I can't wear it tonight. I think that'd be too weird."

"You totally can, and you will. He's a guy; do you think he's going to remember a dress you wore years ago?" she asks. "Plus, there isn't anything about your friendship with Fallon that's ordinary."

I guess she's right. It's just a plain red dress. I walk to the washroom to try it on. When I come out Alex is pouring some more wine. She's looking through the book I made her for the wedding. It's three quarters of the way full now which makes me feel happy, like I've at least accomplished something this past year.

"You look so good! I knew it would fit," she says. "Oh, and check the bag again, there's a box lining the bottom."

I lift the box out from the bag and open it. It's a pair of black shoes with a gold coloured heel. They're perfect.

"I should go out more often if this is what you're going to do for me," I laugh. She laughs too.

"Are you guys going to talk about the wedding rehearsal?" she asks.

"Yeah we can go over that for sure," I say. If I'm being honest, I didn't really have a plan for what Fallon and I are going to discuss. We almost have everything ready for the bachelor and bachelorette parties.

Alex and I talk a little while longer and then she offers to drop me off at the bar. She's staying over for the night so she said I can either Uber back or she'll pick me up. We're taking advantage of the fact that Joey is away. We get in her car and start driving towards the bar.

After a few minutes something inside of me doesn't feel right. I haven't spoken to Joey all day and have a sudden urge to call him.

"Do you mind if I call Joey quickly?" I ask.

"No, not at all," Alex answers.

I pull out my phone and dial his number. It goes straight to voicemail. I try again and he picks up. He sounds like he's been sleeping.

"Hi, honey," I say.

"Hi, how are you? Do you need anything?" he asks. His compassion makes my heart ache. It's sad that I cherish an emotionless sentence so much.

"No, I'm okay. I'm doing well. I'm just at home, about to go to bed. I wanted to call and make sure you're having a good trip," I lie. I see Alex roll her eyes. She pulls over across the street from the bar and parks the car.

"That's good. Get some sleep," he says, trying to forcefully end the conversation.

"Sorry if I woke you, I just wanted to hear your voice," I say.

"That's sweet, we'll talk soon," he says. "Goodnight."

The line cuts. I turn to Alex who has her mouth open in amazement.

"That was the weirdest conversation I've ever heard between a husband and wife," she says flatly.

"I know, I just feel so strange. It feels like I'm cheating on him, seeing Fallon all the time like this," I say with guilt.

"Yeah, that's why you're meeting Jennifer, not Fallon. Honestly though, Jos, unless you actually cross that line, there's nothing to worry about," she says.

I stay silent, unable to say anything because I know I can't contain the truth much longer. I still haven't told her about the night Fallon and I slept together and I can't lie anymore.

"Wait…" she pauses. "Are you kidding me? You guys hooked up? Don't you lie to me, Josephine Parker!" she almost yells.

"It was the night of your party. I hadn't seen him in years and there was so much tension. I've been dying to tell you, but I didn't want to cause any drama. Please don't tell Dan. I feel horrible about it," I beg.

I can see that she's thrilled. "No wonder he grins like an idiot any time I mention you," she laughs.

"I know, he told me he still has feelings for me," I say.

"So, what are you going to do?" she asks.

"That was almost a year ago. He told me he still isn't ready for a relationship and even if I was interested, I'm married. The guilt I'm feeling is horrible; that's why we made the contract," I say.

"The exact same excuse he had back then," she sighs. "I don't know, I think you guys would be perfect together."

I shrug, opening the car door and begin to walk towards the bar. Before I close the door, I look back at her.

"We can talk more about it later. Thank you so much for driving me, and for this dress," I say. I shut the door behind me.

I approach the bar, taking a deep breath as I always do when I'm about to see Fallon. Despite our contract and my guilt when it comes to Joey, seeing Fallon is always nerve racking. I'm not sure why feelings from so long ago hold onto me the way that they do. Fallon is so passionate when he speaks to me that it makes me forget about the rest of the world. It is like a do-over, a second chance. A friendship different than one I've ever had. I push through the door and the hot air inside hits me. I see a crowd of people sitting at a table by the bar. They're a familiar looking bunch. As I look closer, I see Fallon... and Dan... and Charlie and the list goes on. Did he forget about our meeting?

As this thought crosses my mind, I feel someone tap my shoulder. It's Alex.

"Surprise!" she shouts. This captures the attention of the table and everyone follows, "Happy Birthday!"

"I probably gave it away by driving you here, but Fallon set this up weeks ago. He wanted to give you a surprise party. It's nothing crazy, but I know that's just what you like," she says hugging me.

Fallon walks up behind her and she detaches from our hug. He's looking a lot more put together than when I last saw him. His hair is pulled back and he's wearing a deep blue suit.

"Happy birthday, Josephine," he says hugging me.

"Thank you, you didn't need to do this. But, thank you," I smile.

I then become subject to countless "happy birthdays" and hugs. I feel my guard go down, unlike when I'm at home. I'd forgotten all about my birthday until Alex brought it up at my house. I don't even know how Fallon remembered. Dan grabs everyone a round of drinks and they make me do one of those shots filled with whipped cream. We all get a good laugh and then everyone breaks up into small groups. I quickly realize that there isn't anyone here, besides my friends.

"Why aren't there any other people here?" I ask Dan.

"This guy booked the place out," he says throwing his arm around Fallon. I can tell Dan's drunk already, I'm sure they all came early to pre-game.

"Fallon!" I say in awe. I keep forgetting how wealthy everyone in my life is.

"Oh, it's nothing," he says. "I just hope you enjoy the night."

In all the years I've known Joey he hasn't ever done anything like this. Thinking back, he's never even thrown me a birthday party.

I head over to see the girls. Everyone from the wedding party is here, except for Jade. Charlie says that she's gotten her morning sickness at night so far during the pregnancy. I'm surprised that he isn't at home taking care of her.

"Thank you all for coming," I say. "Are you ladies excited for the bachelorette party?"

"Hell yes! I've never been to a resort like that before," Emily says.

"I actually went there once with my husband, we hated it. They say it's supposed to be quiet and relaxing, but it's full of partiers. We couldn't escape the crowds of people," Abigail adds.

"Oh, shut up Abi. You're just mad because your husband's a prude. Can't please this one," Alex says, trying to gloss over Abigail's comment.

"It was hard to find a spot everyone would like, but this is what Alex wanted," I say defensively. I can see myself having a problem with Abigail already; she seems so judgemental.

"Are the guys excited?" Jessica asks.

"Dan says they are. They're staying on the opposite side of the resort from us," Alex answers.

"Are any of you bringing your boyfriends or husbands?" I ask.

"My husband's working," Abigail replies. "*And thank god for that,*" I think.

"Emily and I are single, so we're pumped! No guy can resist twins," Jessica says.

"Josie and I know that," Alex says. She looks at me and laughs. She's thinking of the twins that we went on a double date with in college.

"Do you girls know if Fallon's single?" Jessica asks.

I choke a bit on my drink. I don't know why that shocks me so much; he's a very attractive man.

"I think he might be into me. At Josie's party he had his hands all over me, but he never initiated anything. When we went to head home I thought he would invite me over but he just ordered us separate cabs. He's so hot though, I know with a bit of time I can win him over," she says confidently.

"Yeah, he's single," Alex smiles. "But I am not sure if blondes are his type".

"Oh, he'll like you. Charlie actually told me that he only dates blonde girls," Emily corrects her.

"That's funny. I'm not sure we should be trusting Charlie's opinion," Alex says.

It's almost midnight. I know this because Alex keeps reminding me every five minutes. I can't believe I almost forgot my own birthday. If they hadn't put this together, I probably would have gone all day tomorrow not knowing.

Fallon walks up and cuts the conversation short.

"Hey ladies, I got the keys to the kitchen and brought stuff to make burgers. Anyone want one?" he asks.

"I'll have one," Jessica says batting her eyes. *Of course* she wants one.

"Why don't you just make all of them, I'm sure I'll want one in an hour or so," Alex suggests.

"Good idea," Fallon replies. "Hey, do you want to come and help me?" he asks, nudging my shoulder.

"Why not," I shrug.

I put down my cup and follow him into the kitchen. He turns a key into the wall to activate the lights.

"I don't know if you know this about me, but I actually used to be a cook before I went to pilot school," he says as he pulls the ingredients from the fridge. "Can you hand me that bowl under the countertop?" he asks.

"I sure can, and no, you've never told me that. I don't know if you know this about yourself or not, but you're not the easiest person to get to open up," I reply, this comment makes him laugh.

"I know. I'm sorry about that..." he trails off. "Now, let me teach you how to make the world's best burger."

"Alright," I smile and follow along.

We stand across from each other. Step-by-step he shows me how to make the patty. It's pretty fun. I can't believe I've never done this before. I look at him for a moment and forget about our contract. I remember what Alex told me at the party about his parents and I want to ask him about them so badly. I just don't want to ruin another moment. He's the perfect man and I wish I could tell him that without coming off like I am trying to get in his pants. He needs to know that what happened isn't his fault. I try to communicate that without any words, but it doesn't seem to work.

"Josie," he looks up at me.

"Yes, Fallon," I reply.

"Happy birthday," he smiles. "Oh, and I really like your dress."

"Thank you," I say flushing. I guess he *does* remember it.

I would have killed to spend a birthday with Fallon years ago; this moment seems to make up for it. I begin to get the condiments ready for everyone and Fallon leaves the kitchen to grab the bag of buns that he left out on the bar counter.

I check my phone to see if I have a text from Joey: I don't. He's never not wished me a happy birthday. He usually calls me once the clock strikes twelve if he's out of town. I'm convinced he's forgotten so I slide my phone into my purse.

"Is everything okay?" Fallon asks walking back into the room.

"Yeah, it's perfect actually," I say. If Joey has forgotten me, then I'm going to do the same. I can't let him ruin this night for me. I stand beside Fallon as he turns on the grill. We place the burgers on to the heat and he teaches me how to cook them.

Chapter Thirteen

one month until the wedding...

Today is the day of Alex's bachelorette party. Fallon and I decided to rent a bus to take everyone to the resort. We're all standing in a bus station parking lot at an equidistant location from most of our houses. I brought everyone coffee from my favourite coffee shop. Alex told me it's not as good as hers so I decided that I would bring enough for everyone and let them decide. I begin to hand out the coffee and the bus pulls up in front of us.

Everyone is dressed down, except for me; they are all in sweatpants, sweatshirts and running shoes. I guess I didn't get the memo.

"It's going to be a long ride, are you sure you don't want to change?" Alex asks one last time before we get on.

"I'll be fine," I say handing her a cup and getting on the bus.

I sit at the very back and Alex slides in beside me, even though there's an entire empty bus and less than ten people on it. Dan slides in across from us and Fallon sits in front of Dan. Charlie and Jade take the seats in front of Fallon. I'm surprised that Jade is coming since she's super pregnant. From what Alex tells me though, I wouldn't leave Charlie alone with a bunch of girls either. Their relationship has been rocky for as long as we've known them.

It's a quiet ride up because everyone has fallen asleep. I feel bad that the bus driver is stuck by himself at the front. I don't feel bad enough to part the group and sit with him though.

The clothes I'm wearing are becoming uncomfortable, and I want to sleep, but I have a difficult time sleeping in moving vehicles. I look up at Fallon. His head is propped on the window and his legs are spread across to the seat beside him. He's asleep with hand tucked beneath his chin. He looks so serious and peaceful all at once. How can someone be so complicated, yet almost perfect? I try to shake this thought from my mind, but I keep getting pulled back in. Three hours with nowhere to go and nothing to do will do that to a person. He's different each time I see him. He's wearing a tight white shirt and grey sweats. I look closer at his shirt, lifting myself up to read the front, trying not to wake Alex. He's wearing the t-shirt he wore the day we met. He truly must have remembered my dress the other night. I smile and sit back down. My mind races for the rest of the ride.

We arrive at the resort. A giant yellow bus stands out from the limos slung around the side of the front entrance. We file out, everyone still waking up from their naps. It feels like I'm back in college being surrounded by the people from my past life. The one I had before marriage.

Fallon and I check everyone in and we make plans to meet at a club that's only a short trolley ride from our hotel rooms. Alex and Dan aren't supposed to be near each other this weekend, but they're so infatuated with one another that I doubt it will last. The girls and I begin to walk back outside and wait for a trolley to pick us up.

"This place doesn't actually seem that bad," Abigail says as she looks around.

"Glad you approve," I reply. I'm getting tired of her smartass remarks. I worked so hard on this weekend for Alex and she doesn't need one of her friends ruining it for her.

"Wait until you see the rooms. They looked so nice online," Alex says.

A trolley pulls up to us and we file on. Jade sits up front with the driver, just to be safe. She's pretty far along in her pregnancy and we want to keep her as safe as possible. A cart pulls up across from us for the guys and they climb in. We pull off in opposite directions, waving each other off as we go. As we pull up to the building we're staying in, we grab our bags and head inside. We're on the first of 15 floors. I've never been to a resort with so many rooms. I figured that the best bet for a bunch of drunken women would be to refrain from using the stairs and keeping things as simple as possible. The ground floor also happens to be the only one that has joint rooms. I hand out room keys and the girls head into their rooms. We all file in and unlock the doors attaching our rooms. Alex and I are sharing the first room, beside us is Jade, followed by Abigail, Jessica and Emily.

After splitting up the rooms we decide that we'll go for dinner just us girls for the first night. Everyone starts to shower and do their hair and makeup. I'm excited to get to know the girls better. Since marrying Joey I've hardly had time to do anything other than cater to him. I haven't hung out with Jade since meeting her simply because of her ties to Fallon. I bet she'll have a lot to say about Charlie. They've broken up and gotten back together more times than I can count on two hands. They've been together for so long with no sign of marriage. She must be getting frustrated with him by now.

Emily and Jessica are at our door saying that they want to have pre-drinks. It's only 6:00p.m. and yet they're ready to start. I can already tell that tonight's going to be an interesting one. Emily's bubbly and chatty. She hasn't had a drink yet but she's talking way more than usual.

Once Abigail and Jade come into the room, Emily starts passing out shots. All of us, except for Jade, take one and toast to an amazing weekend ahead. Just as we're all finally ready to go to our reservation, Emily stands up and blurts out that she's been dying to tell us something.

"I met someone" she says cheerfully. "We've been talking non-stop since right after Josie's party. I met him for the first time a few weeks ago. We met at this cute little cafe and sat talking for hours."

I automatically feel happy for her; at least someone should be enjoying their love life right now.

"Emily, I'm so excited for you," Alex says hugging her sister. Emily hasn't been on a date in at least two years. The twins are a few years older than Alex, so she's always making sure they put themselves out there. And when they're excited over guys, she makes sure she is too.

"Can we see a picture of him?" I ask, joining in on their excitement. I've always considered Alex's sisters as my own. It makes me sad that we haven't spent a lot of time together since college.

"Yes, I'll pull up his dating profile," she says pulling out her phone. She turns to Alex and starts swiping through his pictures one by one. "I just have a really good feeling about him. He's so charm-," she starts as Alex cuts her off.

"You're kidding me, right? Emily are you joking with us?" she shouts, grabbing Emily's phone and handing it to me.

"What's wrong?" she asks.

After looking at the phone screen I place the phone down on the table beside me. I don't say anything, I just turn and walk into the bathroom. I'm not surprised that Joey has been cheating on me. I'm just surprised that the girl I saw him with at the cafe was my best friend's sister. I know that Alex's sisters have never met Joey; he didn't interact with any of my friends at his party besides Alex and Dan. I'm still so confused as to how this happened.

I shut the door softly behind me and lift the toilet seat to puke. This hurts a lot more than it did when I saw him at the cafe. Alex comes up to the door and asks me if I'm okay.

"I'm sorry," she says through the door. "I knew that Joey was a scumbag, but I didn't realize he was capable of this." She doesn't even know the half of it.

After a few minutes I open the door slowly to see Alex in the room alone. My makeup has been completely washed down my face from my tears. She greets me with a huge hug and I let go of some sobs that have been sitting inside of me for a while now. Each day that passes I learn to hate Joey in a new way.

"Where did everyone go?" I ask.

"I asked them if they can meet us at the restaurant," she replies.

"I don't understand how this could happen. I don't know what I'm supposed to do," I say frantically.

"You need to leave him. It's simple, I'll help you," she insists.

"It's not as easy as you'd think," I say. We both sit in silence for a moment.

"Did you tell them?" I ask.

"No, I didn't. I don't feel like that's my place. I want to though. She's my sister, Josie," she says nervously.

"Can we at least wait until after the trip? I need some time to think without having to deal with everyone's opinions," I reply.

"If you're sure that's what you want... So, what do you want to do now? Do you want me to just go pick something up for you to eat?" she asks.

"I'm not really hungry, but we should go meet the girls. I need to get my mind off of this, plus I don't want to ruin this weekend for you," I say shrugging my shoulders.

--

Dinner is awkward. Alex and I haven't told anyone that Joey's my husband. I'm not surprised by a lot anymore. I'm mostly shocked that he's strung so many different women along. His life is an absolute lie and he's making mine become one too. I sip my drink, beginning to despise him more.

"Al, why were you so upset before? Did I do something wrong?" Emily asks.

"I'm sorry. He just looks really familiar," Alex replies slowly, trying to hold in her anger. "I thought he was someone I knew."

"Oh, I see," Emily says, her look of confusion fades into a smile. "Well, good thing he's not!" Alex's explanation seems to make Emily feel more at ease.

I don't talk much as most of the conversation revolves around Emily's new fling. I'm pissed off as the wife of her new boyfriend. She talks about how much of a gentleman he is. How on their first date he told her he was happier than he'd been in years. I don't know if that's more of an insult to myself or to Dana, the nurse he slept with at his party. I see things in Alex's eyes that I've never seen before. The more Emily speaks, the more she looks like she's going to cry. She's pissed and she's having a hard time containing it. She's gotten up to leave three times already and she's just excused herself from the table for a fourth time.

"What's up with her?" Jade asks.

"How many times is that, five? God, she can't have the attention on anyone else for even a moment," Jessica says angrily.

"I don't think it has anything to do with Emily or her new boyfriend," I say sharply. I'm trying to keep Joey's identity unknown. I don't want this weekend to be all about my marital problems more than it already is.

"Yeah you guys, she's not like that," Emily adds. "I bet she's just in an argument with Dan or something…"

Alex comes back to the table and we stop talking about her. We shift the conversation to meeting the guys at the club later.

My phone buzzes on my lap. The girls continue to talk in the background while I look down at my phone's display screen and see the name Jennifer lit up across it. I could have guessed as much.

"How's it going?" Fallon's message reads. He always comes in at the perfect time; when I need a distraction and am on the brink of losing my mind.

"It's okay, but I can bet that your night is going a lot better," I type back.

"We'll we will have to wait and see later. The guys are all wasted. Dan's cousin won't stop talking about Emily," he replies.

"You should tell him she's seeing somebody," I text back, my fingers burning as I type.

"Oh, really? I'm not gonna mention it. He's a few shots in and has courage I've never seen in him before," he texts.

"We'll be there soon," I reply.

I put my phone down and Alex leans over to me.

"I know you said you don't want to, but I think we should tell my sister," she says in my ear.

"Alex, I told you we can't," I say eagerly.

"I would rather her hear it from one of us than from Joey," she says.

"What do you mean, Joey?" I say loudly. The girls have turned their focus to our conversation.

"I called him while I was in the bathroom and told him to stay the hell away from my sister," she says firmly. I can feel tension forming between us, thicker than I have ever felt it before.

"You really shouldn't have done that," I say reaching for my phone. There are about six missed calls and a dozen text messages from Joey lighting up my screen.

217

"Shouldn't have done what?" Abigail says. My dislike for her is growing wildly; her intrusiveness and lack of self-awareness is getting to me. If Alex has the nerve to make my decision for me, then I'm not going to care so much about the fate of this weekend.

"We're just discussing the fact that the Joey Emily's dating is the same Joey that I'm married to," I say flatly.

As the words spew out of my mouth I push back my chair and walk out of the room without looking back. I can hear muffled words trailing behind me followed by a huge sob let out by Emily. I feel horribly for her. I feel even more horribly that I'm not staying behind to explain. Then again, I shouldn't have to explain something that I only just found out myself.

My phone is still buzzing, this time it's Alex.

"Hey," I say, pressing the phone to my ears.

"Please don't be mad, I realize that I shouldn't have called Joey, but she's my sister. You know how much you both mean to me," she explains.

"Now you see what I've been dealing with. You go meet the guys, they're already on their way to the club. I'll be fine," I say.

"Are you going to come?" she asks.

"Yeah," I respond. I'm unsure if I mean this or not.

I grab a drink at one of the outdoor bars and sit across from the club. The lights are dim and the tables are almost empty. I'm shocked at how quiet it is. After half an hour I watch the girls as they pass by without even noticing me. I decide not to reply to Joey, he's far enough away to ignore without immediate consequence. In the distance I see man with dirty blonde hair walk out from the club and light a cigarette. I realize quickly that the man is Charlie. He sees me and begins to wave with his free hand. He walks over and asks if he can sit. I could use the company of someone on the outside.

"I heard what happened," he says. "I'm sorry to hear things aren't going well."

"Thanks, Charlie," I sigh.

"If I'm being honest, I never really liked him," he says.

"You're not the first person to tell me that," I say letting out an obnoxious laugh.

"This might help," he says passing me his smoke.

I take it from him and place it between my lips as he lights another for himself. It's nice to taste a cigarette again even though it's only my second time smoking. I can understand the addiction behind it. It's something comforting in moments of extreme discomfort. He orders us a bucket of beer and we start talking about the night we met.

"It's crazy how much has changed since we met. I mean, you look almost the same but now you're married and-" he begins, but I cut him off.

"And you're about to be a father," I interrupt.

"Yeah, exactly," he laughs.

"I must say, you're more talkative than I remember," I add.

"I hadn't talked to a lot of girls until I met Dan and Fallon. The night you and I met was the first time I had gone out with them. It happens to be the night I met Jade too. Her and I have argued so much over the years, it took the anxiety of talking to girls right out of me," he shakes his head and taps his cigarette against an ashtray.

"Wow, I'm impressed. You've already said more to me than you have in the entire time I've known you," I state.

We both laugh again. He seems different now. Alex and Dan have always told me about how disastrous he's become over the years. I don't see it. Maybe it's the fact that we've each had three beers and some shots since we got here, or maybe everyone just underestimates him. I choose the latter.

"Why don't we go inside? Emily's stopped crying. I saw her making out with Dan's cousin," he says standing up from his chair.

"Sure, why not?" I say, I push my chair out to follow.

As we begin to walk to the entrance, Charlie slips his hand in mine. I find this to be very strange; his pregnant girlfriend is right on the other side of the doors. I pull my hand away quietly, just in time for him to reach for the door handle and open it. I want to ask him what that was about, but I let it go for the sake of causing any more drama.

We walk up to the group; half of them are off dancing, but Alex and Dan are sitting in the booth doing shots with Emily and Mark. We slide in beside them.

"Guys, we're doing shots! Take one!" Dan shouts.

"I can see that," I say lightly.

Alex mouths sorry to me from across the table. I nod, showing her I've let any hard feelings go. I can't stay mad at her for too long.

"Can we talk, Josie?" Emily asks.

"Yeah, let's go grab a drink," I say pulling her hand and leading her out of the booth.

We order two drinks and stand facing each other. It's a bit awkward for a moment. At the same time we both say, "I'm sorry."

"Wait, why are you saying sorry? You didn't even do anything," she says in disbelief.

"I know I didn't, but Joey did. I know how blinding his love can be. You seemed so happy, I didn't want to be the one to wreck it for you," I say apologetically.

"I should be the only one apologizing. I've known you for so long and I had no idea that he was your Joey. I feel like an idiot. Bragging about him in your face like that," she says looking away.

"It's okay. How could either of us have known?" I shrug.

She hugs me and walks off to join Mark. Charlie takes her place standing in front of me. He seems a bit more intoxicated than he did thirty minutes ago. He slips his hand around my waist and pulls me in. I awkwardly stumble and land overtop of his crotch. I realize that was his intention and I cringe. He wasn't trying to be a friend to me, he was only trying to pull a move on me like he did the night I met him. I don't see Jade anywhere around, but I'm extremely uncomfortable. I push away from him.

"I don't know what I could have said to give you the impression that I'm into you, but I'm not," I say.

"Oh come on, don't be a tease. I know you've wanted me since we met," he says brushing his hand behind my hair and pulling me in to kiss him.

My body stands still as I turn my head away from him and his mouth lands on my neck. My eyes look across the room at Dan sitting in the booth and he starts to get up. He looks angry, but even more furious is the hand that yanks Charlie by his shirt and punches him in the face. The hand belongs to Fallon.

"What the fuck, man?" Charlie says holding his hand over his eye.

"Don't you ever touch her again!" Fallon screams. I've never seen him like this before.

"Dude, what do you want me to do? Wait around for another five years like you did?" Charlie mocks.

"You can do whatever you want. You should just remember that you have a baby on the way and Josephine is married," Fallon says clenching his teeth. His eyes are burning. They look like they could set fire.

"Whatever," Charlie scoffs, "didn't stop you."

His words invite Fallon's hand in once more and he knocks Charlie out cold. Fallon takes off and he stops outside to hand the bouncer a bundle of money. The bouncer pats him on the shoulder and Fallon fades out of sight.

I stumble back and land sitting on a bar stool. All I wanted was a weekend without being the centre of attention. Yet here I sit, waist deep in it.

Chapter Fourteen

It's the second day at the resort. The girls and I are sitting on the floor playing Would You Rather like we're in high school again. There's not much else to do considering last night's events. None of the girls are upset with me; they just sit awkwardly in the middle of it all. Charlie, Jade, Abigail and Mark all left this morning. It's just Fallon, Dan, Alex, the twins, and I still here. It's been a horrible start to what's supposed to be Alex and Dan's last few weeks of freedom. It's 7:00p.m. and the girls and I have already eaten dinner. We called room service for burgers, fries, and pizza. I haven't spoken to Charlie or Fallon since last night and I have no idea what took place after I left. I just hope Fallon's okay.

I got Joey on the phone as soon as I left the club. He was very calm, which makes me nervous for the next time I see him. He told me that what happened between him and Emily could be explained and ended the call fairly quickly. I think he was so calm because he didn't know who was around me at the time. It makes me wonder what would've happened if I'd confronted him at home.

I usually wonder what it would be like if I'd chosen a different path rather than what I have now with Joey, but all of this chaos makes me want to crawl back into the hole that is our life together.

"Would you rather go skinny dipping with Fallon or Charlie?" Emily asks interrupting my thoughts. I realize that nobody knows about Fallon and I besides Alex.

"Hmm, that's a good one. I've always had a thing for blond guys, but Fallon's sexy. I mean it's Fallon Adams; the most unobtainable guy on the history of the planet. Plus, if he's willing to knock out a guy for someone he hardly knows, I wonder what he would do for someone he was dating," Jessica responds.

"I'd say Fallon too," Alex says in agreeance.

"Al!" I say shocked.

"What? Fallon's hot. Dan knows he's totally my type," she laughs, shoving a handful of fries into her mouth.

"What about you, Josie?" Jessica asks.

"I'd say Charlie," I lie. Charlie is absolutely repulsive. After he grabbed me last night, I decided to never spend a moment alone with him again.

"I was thinking about asking him out," Jessica says breaking the conversation.

"Who, Fallon or Charlie?" Alex asks.

"Fallon, duh," Jessica replies.

"You guys would be so cute together," Emily says. "You two could double date Mark and I. He told me that he's going to set something up when we all get back to reality. He only lives a few towns over from us."

"Are you not upset about the whole Joey thing?" Alex asks. "That did just happen yesterday…"

"Yeah, it sucks, but Joey wasn't the only guy I've been talking to. I like to keep my options open. I feel worse about what Josie's going through," she says. I reach out and touch Emily's hand in appreciation.

"Don't worry about me, I'll figure everything out," I say softly.

The conversation has fallen flat. The girls are all a little too drunk and there's no sign of them stopping. Alex steps out for a smoke. I can't imagine how stressed she is right now. Her wedding's so close and all I've done is cause her stress. I feel terrible about it. She puts on a sweater and slips out of the back door. I follow behind her.

"Dan said that Fallon and Charlie are good now," she says as she lights up the cigarette and presses it to her lips.

"Oh, really?" I'm genuinely shocked. The way Fallon acted last night made me think they'd never talk again.

"Yeah, apparently he owes Fallon a bit of money. So Fallon decided he'll stick out that friendship until he's paid back. I've never seen him so angry before," she says looking out at the rain.

"Me either," I agree. "Charlie was grabbing me and wouldn't let go. He kept kissing my neck. It was disgusting."

"I hope you're okay, Jos. I didn't realize he was such a creep. It makes sense as to why Fallon got so upset," she replies putting her arm around my shoulder.

"I should have known. I feel bad for Jade though," I say.

"Don't; this isn't the first time Charlie's done this kind of thing to her. I've told her too many times to leave that guy," she says falling flat. I think we both realize how similar the situation between Charlie and Jade is to Joey and I.

"Anyways, I think I'm going to grab a walk before bed," I say. "It's going to be a long drive back tomorrow."

"Are you sure? I think the rain is only going to pour harder," she asks.

"Yeah, I need to clear my mind," I turn to walk down the steps.

"Okay, stay safe," Alex says.

"Thanks. And Al, I'm sorry this weekend sucked. Fallon and I tried so hard to make it perfect," I say, not looking her in the eye.

"It's surely going to be memorable and isn't that what bachelorette parties are all about?" she grins.

"You're absolutely right," I smile back at her.

I walk down a lit path to the back of the resort. It's so quiet here. It's like the fallouts that occurred between our friend group changed the mood of the entire place. My sandals squish along the damp rocks. It's been raining all day. I stop at a bar and grab a drink, walking and sipping, trying to get my mind off of my life. It seems that the further I get from my home, the more my life comes undone. It's fallen apart more so now than ever before. I decide in my mind that I'm going to go home to Joey. I can't end up like Charlie and Jade; unmarried and pregnant, starting life over by the time I'm in my mid-thirties.

The rain begins to thicken, but it's still more of a mist than a pour. There's a line of hot tubs along the side of the beach with roofs hanging over top and they're all lit up with faded blue and purple lights. It's too bad the girls didn't get to come here. As I approach the hot tub I can see Fallon lying in the water, his arms propped out over its edge, a drink in one hand while his other hand is grabbing the side of the tub. His head is hung back over the ledge and his hair is swept behind him. It looks as if he's sleeping, but I can tell he's not. I recognize the lines on his face; I can tell he's in deep concentration. I walk across the hot tub and look at him for a moment. I wonder how long it will take him to notice me here. He looks peaceful; almost like he did when he was sleeping on the bus, but in a slightly different way this time.

"Hi," I say softly.

"Hey," he muffles back, slowly lifting his head up. It seems like he's been drinking. Yesterday must have shaken him.

"What are you doing out here all by yourself? Where's Dan?" I ask.

"I was waiting for you," he says. He sits upright and smiles at me.

"Funny," I laugh. "How are you feeling about yesterday? I'm really sorry if what happened was a result of anything I did."

"Charlie is a pig, Josephine. He was a pig last night and long before that. He heard about what happened with you and Joey and his first thought was to go find you," he says, brushing his thumb over his bruised knuckles.

That thought makes my stomach knot. It makes me glad that we didn't go somewhere more secluded. If he was planning to come and see me, who knows what would have happened if we were alone when he touched me.

"Well thank you. I'm glad that you were there to have my back," I say.

"Someone needs to," he states. "Do you want to come in?"

My mind stirs. I do, but the closer I get to Fallon, the more I want to cross lines that I shouldn't.

"I can't, I didn't bring a swimsuit," I make an excuse. "I don't think anyone would appreciate seeing me in my bra and underwear."

"I think you're wrong; I for one would appreciate that," he says looking at me. "You'd be doing this place a favour; I haven't seen a single person pass by in an hour."

"Okay, fine," I say rolling my eyes. I take off my sweater and shorts then begin to climb in. I sit directly across from him and I think he can feel the distance I'm trying to create. He doesn't say anything about it, he just continues with our conversation.

"I'm glad that what happened with Charlie didn't make you leave," he says.

"Me too," I say, letting my body sink into the warm water. "Alex told me that the only reason you're still talking to him is because he owes you money."

"She told you that?" he asks, sounding surprised. "I bet she didn't tell you Dan owes me money too."

I feel my eyebrows raise. She didn't tell me that.

"That's a story for another day, I doubt she even knows. Don't tell her I told you that. Sorry, I'm a bit buzzed," he says, trying to clean up after himself.

"It's okay, I won't," I assure him. I'm enjoying being this close to Fallon. Our conversation flows like water. He doesn't make me feel timid or scared and I wish the feeling wasn't temporary.

"Have you talked to Joey about what Emily told you?" he asks, bringing the conversation that I'm having in my head to reality.

"Yeah, I called him after I left the club. He said that he was feeling lonely," I say.

I see Fallon tighten. I know that Fallon hates Joey. Most of the time, I do too. It's getting harder and harder to hide the way my life is behind closed doors. I have been thinking about mine and Joey's last big fight; how he pushed me down the stairs and made me lie to a therapist. I almost forgot about that. I usually do, until I'm getting ready in the morning and find myself pouring foundation onto my forearm and ankle from the bruising that was left.

"I try not to speak about it because I know how you feel about people analyzing your life, but that guy's a bastard. I noticed him flirting with some girl at your party all night long, right in front of you. It's sick. I bet you he's sleeping with her too," he says resting his head back.

The water on his chest glows in the light and the lines of his jaw seem endless. He's as handsome as he is honest. That's how a man should be. He's saying the absolute truth, breaking down my walls by not being afraid to tell me how he feels. There's no dancing around it. He hits it on the head every time he speaks.

"He is," I say. I haven't told anyone else that besides Faye. "I walked in on him fucking her in the new car I got him."

"Unbelievable," he says softly, "I'm sorry."

"Can I talk to you about something?" I ask him. The rain behind us begins to pour and I now find myself in the seat to his left. My drink is gone and so are my walls. It's nice to be with someone so receptive, someone who actually hears me.

"Of course," he says placing his hand on my arm.

"Here," I say, putting my forearm under the water and washing rapidly at the makeup covering my cut to remove it. I hold my arm up to him and tears are leaking from my eyes. I'm trying hard to detain them.

"Oh god, Josie," he gasps. "You told me you'd call me if it gets worse."

"I know," I say feeling a pang of guilt in my chest. "We got into an argument and he pushed me. I don't think he meant for me to fall; I think I tripped over my own feet," I'm glossing over the fact that the fight started because I told Joey I was meeting my mom when I was busy on the phone with Fallon.

"Nobody should get that upset. Please tell me you're leaving him. He's not going to change," he says, wrapping his arms around me.

He pulls me into a hug. Not a sideways one this time. A hug like the one we shared five years ago when I found him crying on the balcony. I feel pain in my heart for the way he felt and still feels every day. Maybe that's why we're so good together; we're both broken. His damp hands move up and into my hair and he's holding the back of my head, bringing it toward him. I don't flinch at his touch. Instead, I fall into it. I feel myself sinking in love. The time I've spent forcing myself into friendship has washed away. I think that I'm in love with him and it's devastating to know that as long as I am with Joey, I can never have Fallon in the way that I want to.

I pull away and move myself onto his lap. I trace the edges of his face with my hand. He's soft, yet strong. His eyes are crying tears for me. They are silent and forceful. My hands fall from his face to his lips, the same song and dance we did outside of my house. I pull back for a moment.

"What about just friends?" I ask. "I thought we had a deal?"

"Josie, I meant it when I said I love you. Two people can't just be friends if one of them loves the other," he sighs.

I place my thumb on his mouth to stop him from speaking then replace it with my lips. I can't fight the force of his words and my feelings for him. He represents the life I could've had; the happiness my twenty-year-old self desperately craved. We kiss softly and slowly. His hands find their way down my body, pulling me in with a strong force. His touch is filled with desire and pain. I don't want it to end. I know that the warmth of his mouth and lips will never be matched. His kisses trail down my face, replacing all of the drunken and hateful kisses left by Joey.

He takes the straps of my bra and pulls them off of my shoulders. His hands then grab at its clasp, unhooking it and sliding it off. He wants to feel what is underneath, and so he does. He seems more prepared this time, as if he's been thinking about it in his mind. He pulls at the sides of his swimming trunks, rolling them down off of his body and I begin to touch him. He isn't hiding how it makes him feel. His face is showing each moment of pleasure. I've missed him so much.

"Turn around," he whispers.

His hand feels the sides of my body as he presses himself into me. I'm holding myself up by the ledge of the hot tub and he's inside of me. He's trying to control his pace but I can tell he's having difficulty. I hold the side of his leg with my free hand, as he quickens. I don't think he's able to control himself any longer. I ask him to stop because I want to look at him. He turns and sits, as I get on top and straddle him, turning him on even more. I scale his body as I move on him. I'm not sure if we'll ever get this moment back. He then pulls me into him, his hand fitting into the small of my back and the other holding my head again.

"Josie," he whispers into my ear. "Please come home with me."

I kiss him hard. We both know that I can't, and I won't. I feel him release and his head falls back. He pulls me down beside him and I rest my head on his chest while we look out to the water. We are just as silent as the night is around us. We don't speak or dare to move. We are soaking in every second we have together.

"Close your eyes for a moment," he says breaking the silence between us.

I comply, letting myself become more emotionally venerable than I was just moments ago.

"I want you to picture starting over; nothing behind you or ahead of you. No obligations holding you down. No fear or regret, or even hope. If you started over right now and you had the right to choose what your life became, tell me what that would be like?" he asks.

My eyes are closed and all I see is black. As I focus more and more, I can see light in the distance. As I get closer to it, I see Fallon. A super cut of memories unmade flashing through my mind; memories full of life, and memories too devastating to recall dance around me. Thoughts of children, sharing a home, starting my own business, and surrounding ourselves with friends cloud my mind. It hurts because it's what I've always wanted. It looks and feels like the past two hours I've spent here with Fallon without the lingering feeling that it's going to come to an end. I don't answer him. I don't tell him any of it. It's too hard to say when I know that it won't happen.

"I know you won't say it, no matter how badly I want you to. But for me, it looks like a life with you," he says.

Chapter Fifteen

It's quiet this morning. There's half the amount of people on the bus than what we came here with. I think we're all tired from the long weekend we had. I've been thinking about Fallon all morning. After we slept together last night we talked a lot about Joey. I told him that I haven't told anyone else about the abuse. Fallon told me that he thinks I need to leave Joey. If I left, I don't know where I would go or what I would do; I can't imagine starting my life over. The only person who I would want to do that with is Fallon.

I don't feel guilt when I think of Fallon and I anymore. It's hard to feel guilt when you're bruised head to toe by the man who's supposed to protect you. I'm sitting in front of Fallon on the bus this time so that I'm not tempted by his tight shirts and baggy sweatpants. The drive passes by quickly this way.

I have more to think of now than I did on the way up; I found out my husband's cheating on me with my best friend's sister; Charlie tried to take advantage of me; and I slept with Fallon. I shouldn't ever go away again.

I know that Joey won't be home until the weekend. It's now Monday morning, so I have time to get myself back together and shake off any thoughts of Fallon. I don't really want to though. If I'm being honest, his touch makes me feel more alive than I've felt in a long time. I think about the advice Fallon gave me. He told me last night to get an apartment near my mom's house. Well, he actually told me to stay with him if I was going to leave Joey, but I told him I couldn't do that. Living on my own wouldn't be so bad. The only issue would be making it out without a fight after divulging that I want to leave. I've gone back and forth so many times it's exhausting.

The bus pulls into the parking lot where it picked us up only two days ago. Alex and Dan are going to drive me back home, so I put my suitcase into the trunk of their car. We say goodbye to everyone and part ways. I hop into the backseat and Alex begins to drive. Alex and Dan haven't spoken much today, and their mood has transferred into the car ride on the way back to my house. We drive for little over half an hour before I break the silence.

"Did you guys enjoy the weekend?" I ask.

"It was interesting," Dan says. I can tell he's joking, however he comes off seriously.

"How about you, Al?" I ask.

"Yeah, it was good," she says, keeping her eyes on the road.

It feels like a wall has gone up between the three of us and I hate it. My initial reaction is to ignore it. I'd be upset too if my bachelorette party was ruined by my best friend. I ignore my initial instinct and ask her directly what's going on.

"I thought that we were okay. You said to me that you weren't upset about what happened this weekend with Charlie and the stuff with Emily," I say with confusion.

"It's not that at all," she replies flatly.

"Hey, don't you think you two should have this conversation when I'm not here?" Dan asks her.

"No, we're doing this now," Alex replies, her voice breaks. "I don't get it, Josie. I've been your friend longer than anyone else and you don't think you can open up to me about what's going on at home? How many times have I asked you to please let me know if Joey's hurting you?"

"Alex, what are you talking about?" I ask, raising my voice. I'm angry because I know exactly what she's talking about. Fallon told her what I told him in confidence last night; something that I was not ready to talk to her about.

"Listen, I know Alex is upset right now and she's not going to say the right things. We just wish you could have opened up about Joey. You know you always have a home with us. The fact that you would rather stay with that lying douche is what's getting her so emotional," Dan says trying to remain calm.

"I don't know where you got this information from, but you're wrong. Joey may be a cheater, but he's not hurting me. You guys are out of line," I shout.

I'm infuriated. I thought that Fallon was a noble guy but he's a liar. He knew exactly what he was doing last night. From the moment I told him that Joey pushed me, he knew he was going to tell Alex. He had sex with me because he knew I'd never come back to him once he told her. If he loved me like I thought he did, he wouldn't want to ruin my life. I pull out my phone from my pocket and block "Jennifer" from my contact list. I can't forgive Fallon for this.

"Give me a fucking break, Josephine," Alex says with a scoff. "That man has you delusional. If you don't leave him or let us help you, I don't know how much longer I can sit around and watch this."

Her words hurt. Alex and I have never gotten into an argument like this, let alone thought of calling off our friendship. I don't want to let this happen, yet I sit silently back in my seat and endure a quiet hour drive home. Nothing is said and nothing is done. I feel our friendship deflating and I can tell that it's making Dan uncomfortable.

"Please just talk to her, she doesn't mean what she's saying," Dan begs me through a text message.

"I appreciate it, Dan, but she said what she said. If she wants space, she can have it," I reply.

I start texting Joey. I tell him that I miss him and ask him to change his flight schedule to tomorrow. He declines and I'm not surprised by that. I truly have nobody. I'm alone.

Alex's car pulls up to the front of my house. I'm having a difficult time containing my anger, so I remain silent as I leave the car. I don't thank Alex for driving me and I don't tell them goodbye; I just grab my belongings and walk towards my house without looking back. I open my front door and I hear her car pull off. I can tell she's upset by the ferocity she uses when driving away. The wheels spin beneath her car against the rubble before it moves and I realize that I could say anything to stop her in the second before she drives off, but I don't.

I step into my house. It's empty and spotless. It looks just as it did when we bought it. It was untouched by a family back then as it's untouched by a family now. I leave my bag by the door and curl into the couch. I cry tears so

hard that my breathing thickens. I get up to walk over to
the fridge and grab my inhaler out of the basket above it.
I breathe it in a few times and grab a glass of water to
wash the anxiety down. My wrist feels too heavy to hold
my cup, but somehow, I do. I feel absolutely alone. More
so than I did the first time Joey hit me. I walk up the
stairway once I catch my breath and as I reach the top, I
lay my fingers along the railing where my arm was cut
open and blood was shed. There's still some blood
underneath the section of the railing where a loose nail
hangs. I want so badly to throw my body down these
steps again. *What's wrong with me?*

I've suddenly forgotten why I was even going upstairs
and sit down on the landing. I lay my head down, where
it rested after Joey pushed me. I close my eyes and blink
out tears. I don't know how long I lay there, but by the
time I open my eyes again they're burning so hard that I
don't think I could cry another tear if I tried.

Chapter Sixteen

the night before the wedding...

I haven't spoken to Alex or Fallon since the weekend of the bachelor parties. Dan texted me a few times, begging me to call her but I told him that if she wanted to talk, she would need to call me. Besides, since Joey came back from his trip he's become strict again with where I can and cannot go. It's almost as if he knows that other people know what he's doing.

"Are you sure I should wear white?" I ask Joey once more before we leave. I turn to the mirror beside the front door and clip earrings on. I know quite well that you're not supposed to wear white to any sort of wedding-based event, but Joey insisted that I wear this specific dress.

"No, you look great," Joey says. "Before we go, I have something I want to give you."

He walks up to me and pushes my hair to one side. He slides a beautiful necklace with gems the colour of our birthstones around my neck. It's thoughtful and unusual of him; the gesture makes me feel hopeful. I don't know if he's still seeing those other women, but I've convinced myself that it's none of my business; I should just ignore it. Lots of marriages have secrets. Ours can too.

"It's beautiful, Joey," I say giving him a kiss on the cheek.

"Now let's go have fun, and don't forget their gift," he says pointing down at the table beside the front door.

We head outside and are greeted by cool spring winds. I hope that this weather doesn't carry into tomorrow for the wedding. We get into Joey's car and he puts the key in the ignition to start it. Our GPS tells us that it'll take an hour to get there. He chooses to take the back roads which adds an extra half an hour; I don't mind. I need time to think about what I'm going to say to Alex, if I even decide to speak to her. As soon as that thought enters my mind, I shake it out. She's my best friend and it's her wedding rehearsal; of course I'm going to speak to her. I'm just worried about what will happen if Alex and Dan say something to Joey. When I spoke to Dan, he promised me that nothing would be said to Joey about how they feel as long as I assure them that things are better. I'm also worried because Emily's going to be there too. Joey told me that he spoke with her in private after he returned from his trip. The thought of a private meeting between himself and any woman builds an unease within me.

Jade and Charlie are not going to be there because Jade had the baby only a few days ago; a beautiful little girl named Stella. Joey and I laughed about how common that name is. It was the first time we had laughed together in a while.

"I hope you're okay with us taking the back roads," Joey says while rolling up his window.

"Yes, I'm fine with that," I say cautiously.

"Okay, good. There's something I want to talk to you about," he says.

My mind races with all of the things he could want to talk about. What does he know? I don't know if I can stand an hour and a half of his yelling. I take a deep breath and wait for it to begin. He turns to me with a sorrowful expression; something I've not seen on him in years. His eyes swell with water and I can see he's trying not to cry. I don't know what's going on.

"My parents are getting a divorce," he says flatly. "God, I don't know why I'm crying right now. I hardly ever see them, but something about it is making me reflect on us."

"that's terrible, hon" I say softly, brushing my hand against his knee.

"I recognize that things haven't been so good between the two of us lately and I think that we should see a marriage counsellor," he lets out.

My heart lifts again. It hasn't moved for him in a long time and I wasn't sure it still knew how to. He's just given me hope for us, he's given me a reason to stay. I release all of the fear of starting over and leaving him. Those are the words I've always wanted to hear. I swore to myself if he ever moved past his ego and said those nine words to me, that I would stay.

"You have no idea how much that means to me," I say, my fingers move from his knee and wrap around his free hand.

"I don't want to end up like my parents," he sighs. "What about when we have kids? I think you need to work on yourself so we can do that someday. Divorce isn't an option. I want to help you get better for our future."

My hopes come crashing back down: he's just admitted that he thinks *I'm* the problem.

He's the one who neglects me.
He's the one who keeps me from my family.
He's the one who hurts me.

Nothing that I've done justifies the way he abuses me. Not even the fact that I've slept with Fallon. It's an impossible reality to ignore.

"If that's how you see things then maybe we should," I say, removing my hand from his and sinking back into the seat.

--

An hour later we arrive at the rehearsal dinner and the parking lot has only a few cars in it. It's crazy that tomorrow around this time, Alex and Dan will be married. I'm so happy for them, but at the same time I'm sad because I haven't spoken to Alex since our fight. Joey and I walk into the reception hall and to the section that's closed off for the ceremony. The décor is already laid out and it's beautiful; just like Alex's vision book. The colours are so elegant, I know they're going to match her dress perfectly. Everything is in place except for the flowers and cake which will be brought in tomorrow. I walk around with Joey, showing him all of the things that I chose for the wedding. He seems impressed and genuinely interested. I'm not sure if he's only acting like a normal husband because he doesn't really know anyone in the wedding party, but I'm trying to embrace it. I see Dan walk in from the doorway.

"It looks amazing, doesn't it?" he calls.

"It's beautiful. Congratulations again," Joey says.

"Thanks, man," Dan says, giving Joey a handshake. He then turns to me and gives me the biggest hug. I can tell Dan's trying hard to keep things casual with Joey for the sake of our friendship.

"It's so good to see you. Thank you for coming," Dan says pausing. "Would you mind if I spoke with you for a minute, Jos?" Dan asks with a smile.

"She's all yours," Joey says answering for me.

Dan and I walk over to the side, leaving Joey to stand by himself for a moment.

"I know that I said I'd pretend things were fine with Joey, but I'm not gonna lie, I didn't think you'd bring him," Dan says, rubbing the back of his neck.

"What do you mean?" I ask. He should have said something beforehand.

"I didn't tell Alex because I thought you'd change your mind. You know what, its fine. Let me go talk to her," he says walking off.

I walk back over to Joey trying not to show the confusion that I'm feeling inside. We talk for a few minutes about his work until Dan reappears.

"Well, Alex and the team will be here in just a moment. We're going to run through the ceremony quickly and then eat dinner," he says touching my shoulder. My stomach begins to knot at the idea of Alex having a bad reaction to Joey being here tonight.

"Sounds great," I say nervously.

--

I watch Emily and Mark enter the room holding hands. I guess he meant it when he said he would call her back and I'm glad that he did, they make a cute couple. They both wave to me and take seat in chairs near the front of the room. They completely ignore Joey, making it clear that they don't approve of what he did to Emily. Behind them follows Abigail and her husband, Jack. They're very simple looking people. I figure that Jack's either just as annoying as Abigail or a godsend for putting up with her. Next enters Jessica who is followed by Fallon. I guess they're together and this realization stings. The last time I saw him he told me he loved me and I thought I loved him too. After I deleted his number, Fallon never tried reaching out. Now I'm here with my husband and he's here with Jessica. We are all back where we started; pretending to be strangers.

Fallon walks Jessica to Emily and Mark, completely ignoring us as well.

"What's up with them?" Joey asks me.

"Not sure," I say flatly. I can feel myself boiling inside. Tomorrow is going to be extremely awkward if half of the wedding party isn't speaking to me.

Alex walks in with the officiant and her wedding planner. She gives Joey and I a half-smile and stands beside Dan. They explain to us how the ceremony will play out. The men line up alongside Dan and the women head into the hallway. All of the spouses' head into the dining area and grab a drink as they won't be needed for this portion of the evening. I still haven't spoken to Alex and it's making me grow uncomfortable. It's also making me uncomfortable that Jessica and Emily won't shut up about Fallon.

Alex and I stand silently for a moment before it's our turn to walk into the ceremony rehearsal.

"You look nice, Al," I say with a soft smile trying to break the ice.

"I'd say the same to you, but you decided to wear a white dress to my rehearsal," she replies, giving me the same smile in return. I don't say another word and turn back around. I had no idea how upset she was with me.

Traditional wedding music starts playing and we're cued to send in the first bridesmaid. Abigail begins walking, but she moves a little too slowly. She's corrected by Alex's wedding planner on her walk a few times as she makes her way down the aisle. It's funny because she was the one who bragged at the bachelorette weekend about being asked to be in so many weddings before this. Emily's next and I watch as she makes eyes at Mark the whole time she walks. I watch as he shoots her a thumbs-up and I think to myself that about how good he is for her. It's then Jessica's turn to walk in, and I follow before Alex enters. My stomach is turning at the idea of walking into a room where almost everyone despises my husband. As I make my walk down the aisle, I try to think of anything other than what's going on at this moment and feelings of nostalgia enter my mind. It's strange walking into this room because it looks so similar to the way my wedding looked. Joey and I are so far from where we started off it makes me wish he and I could go back to that day and start over.

I remember on my wedding day that there was a brief moment of panic where I wondered if I was making the right decision. I began to think about Fallon and all of those who came before him, in the same way that most people think about what could've been before sealing their fate. On that day, Alex told me that Joey was the one here now and that it was meant to be. I listened to her and I didn't think about Fallon again until I saw him years later. He now stands at front of the wedding hall staring at me intently. I try not to make eye contact with him. He made his choice; he inserted himself into a situation that wasn't his to insert himself in. Now whatever was between us is over.

I make it down the aisle and watch Alex walk. When she gets to the front she holds hands with Dan and I watch her recite her vows. I can feel my anger towards her fading. She needs me and I need her. I'm happy for her and I want her to know that.

Once they're finished, we're all instructed on how to walk back down the aisle. Dan and Alex lead, then Fallon and I follow. We step beside each other, linking arms, while my heart is beating out of my chest in anger and in sorrow. He looks so handsome with his hair pushed back the way it is tonight. He looked just as handsome to me on the bus in his sweatpants. He's a good person, but the closer I keep him, the more destructive he becomes to me. He doesn't say a word to me as we walk back down the aisle. Instead, he holds my arm loosely as if he wants to let go. As soon as we make it down the aisle, he does. He walks right out of the door to the dining room and Jessica follows after him. I figured he would have at least said hello. I consider that he's probably hurting too; he knows that he hurt me. Maybe to him telling Alex was the right thing to do, but I told him in about Joey in confidence. And now I don't trust him.

We all make our way to the dinner table. I'd completely forgotten that Joey was waiting for me. He and I are sitting beside Abigail and Jack. What a treat. An annoying, sour, and expired treat. The funny thing about it is that Joey seems to like them. He and Jack used to go to school together as kids and they won't stop talking about their memories together. I guess Alex and Dan wanted to put the problematic people at one end of the table which clarifies why there are two empty seats for Charlie and Jade.

Dinner is long and dull. I want more than anything to go up to Alex and talk about absolutely anything but she's freezing me out tonight. I sit silently, listening to Joey and Jack drone on and on. When their discussion becomes too boring, I look down the table at Fallon and Jessica to watch them interact with one another. After desert comes Joey and I stay for drinks in the main room. I excuse myself to use the washroom and head out the door. Once I've flushed the toilet, I step out of the stall and Jessica comes crashing in. She steps close to me with an angry look across her face.

"Listen, Fallon told me about what happened between you two," she starts.

I'm confused as to what he's told her; he isn't the type to kiss and tell. He lives a very private life and Jessica has always been the type to over-exaggerate. I know that she likes Fallon and has for a while. If something threatens to stand between that, she's going to snap.

"I don't know what he said to you, but nothing happened," I say, trying to step back.

"Before you met your husband, you two dated. Did you think I wouldn't find out?" she scoffs.

"That was almost six years ago. If Fallon's with you, then I'm sure he likes you," I reiterate.

"Oh, trust me, he assured me that it's over between you two. I have a feeling that you're the one I need to be worried about," she says.

"I wasn't disagreeing with you, Jessica. What's your problem tonight?" I ask. "You haven't spoken one word to me since you got here and now you're corning me in the bathroom like a high schooler."

She then knocks my purse from off of the counter and it spills onto the floor. I've been nothing but nice to Jessica since I met her. I've known her as long as I've known Alex, yet she's acting crazy.

"I saw you last weekend in the hot tub. First your husband uses my sister, and now you're sleeping Fallon in public," she yells.

"Okay, have a great night," I say pushing past her and out of the bathroom. My chest begins to tighten and I realize that a life destroying secret now lies in Jessica's hands. She's as unpredictable as Joey and could go off at any minute. I need to get Joey out of here.

Jessica has always been guy-crazy; it's why she's never had a stable relationship. That's what makes me more irritated with Fallon. After the stunt he pulled telling Alex about Joey, he shouldn't be running his mouth to Jessica. I have a hard time believing that he likes her as much as she likes him; I think he just doesn't want to be alone. He's a man who is unable to commit to the things he wants. Yet he commits to all of the things he doesn't want. He's backwards. I walk up to Joey who is talking to Jack, grab his hand, and proceed to pull him towards Alex and Dan.

"I'm sorry to interrupt you two, but we have to leave," I say.

"Oh, okay. Is everything alright?" Dan asks.

"Yeah, everything is fine. We just have a long drive back and want to get a few things ready before we have to leave in the morning," I say, realizing how good I've become at lying.

"We'll see you two tomorrow," Dan says pulling me in for a hug.

I give Alex a wordless hug. She isn't completely receptive to it, but we both understand that we need to get through tomorrow without fighting. Dan shakes hands with Joey, but Alex doesn't even look in his direction. Joey and I leave without saying goodbye to anyone else. He doesn't ask questions about my sudden urgency to leave. He's so emotionally detached that he can't see when I am upset. He has a horrible sense of social cues.

We begin our drive home and it's completely silent on my end. Joey doesn't stop talking about how much he loved Jack. During the ride home I realize that there's nothing more that I want to do than to talk to Alex about everything that happened since I left her car a few days ago. I want to talk to her, but it's the night before her wedding. She's probably trying to get things ready and get rid of her pre-wedding jitters. I feel like a horrible friend.

I can't shake the fact that we just spent four hours at my best friend's wedding rehearsal and hardly anyone there would even look at me. I begin to think about all of the things wrong with mine and Joey's relationship. The further that he and I drive the more anxiety builds in my chest. I finally have a moment to sit and let what's been happening sink in. I've been so worn down over the years that I feel like I'm only a shell of myself. I can't keep living like this.

I try and think back to where it all began; the first time Joey cheated on me. It was three years ago with our cleaner. I came home early one day to put some groceries away before heading to visit a college friend for lunch. When I came home, I set everything inside and went upstairs to change. When I got up the stairs and entered our room, I could hear a woman moaning. It was horrifying. Joey and I had just gotten married and I was head over heels in love. Again, I didn't say a word. I silently walked away. That time, Joey heard me and chased me down the stairs begging me to stay. I slept at Alex and Dan's place for a month. She saw me at my worst, and I was in an even bigger rut than I had been after meeting Fallon. That's one of the many reasons why she has such low expectations of Joey.

When Joey and I get home, I run a bath for him. This has been the only thing he has kept consistent since I found out he was cheating on me again.

I don't blame Alex for the way she feels about him. The cheating mixed with the stunt he pulled by trying to fight

Dan is a recipe for hatred. I need to get out of the house and call her.

I can't bear the thought that Joey has isolated me from her too. She's the only person that I have left, and I won't let him take her from me. I've decided that I need to find a way to leave him and it can't wait until after the wedding. There are too many secrets and too many lies to move forward like this. We had been standing still for a long time, and now we're moving backwards. I need to get out of our relationship before we crash.

I put on my jogging clothes and start on a walk to clear my mind. I should be with her right now; this fight is so stupid. I look at my phone and see that I already have three missed calls from her. I instantly feel better. I open my phone and call her back.

"Jos, thanks for calling me," she says. "I was just calling to say I'm sorry. You can delete all the voicemails."

"I'm sorry too. I know why you're so upset. If it were the other way around, I would have killed Dan," I say. That thought hits me hard and I realize that I'm a hypocrite.

"I know. I'm even sorrier that I ever made you think I'd give up on you," she says.

"I'm going to leave him," I say for the first time out loud. I am leaving Joey.

"You are? Thank god, Josephine," she says, I hear her voice break.

"Yes, tonight opened my eyes. Things are getting a lot worse and I need to move on. I need to be happy and I'm just miserable. I know in my heart that he is too. If he were happy, he'd never be like this," I say.

"Yes, he would. It's not something that's controllable. You have nothing to do with it. It doesn't matter if it were you or I, or someone on the street. If they were with him long enough, they would be inflicted by his anger too," she says.

We talk for hours as I walk around under faded streetlights. Joey hasn't tried to call me which is unlike him. I'm too consumed in my conversation with Alex to care and although it's dark, I feel lighter than ever. I tell Alex about all of the horrible things that have been going on since last year. I tell her about Joey choking me, about the nurse at his birthday party, and about when he pushed me down the stairs and called my mother to come over. Alex and I then talk about all of the things I'll need to do to start over. The most interesting part is that this new future we talk about has nothing to do with Fallon. I think I was so convinced that if I were to start new, it had to be with him. That's what was holding me back; the thought that I couldn't break free on my own.

We come up with a plan of what to say to Joey. We decide that I'll go home and pack a small suitcase of things for the weekend, and tomorrow morning Alex will

come and pick me up on the way to the wedding. Then
when I come back, Alex and Dan will wait outside while
I tell Joey that I'm done, and that I'm leaving.
On the way back home, I let music blast through my
ears. I haven't done this in a while. It feels good knowing
that this is going to be the last night spent in my home
with Joey. I just need to get through the night as
smoothly as possible. I'm glad that Alex's wedding is
tomorrow; it'll be easier having something to talk to Joey
about this evening. He can usually sense when I'm
nervous or lying.

I walk into the garage, glancing at the car I bought Joey.
My mind flashes to the night I saw him in here with
Dana. I get a chill through my spine. I enter the house
through the same door that he did when I saw him
zipping up his fly at the party. I look up through the
staircase and hear the echoes of moaning, just as I did
the first time I caught him cheating on me. All of these
memoires just reaffirm why I'm leaving in the first place.
It makes me feel disgusted and empowered all at the
same time.

The house is dark; Joey must still be having a bath. I
walk over to the fridge to start prepping breakfast for
tomorrow. I like to get the coffee pot ready and scramble
the eggs the night before on a weekend. Monday to
Friday Joey likes his eggs fried, and on the weekends, he
likes them plain and scrambled. As I whisk the milk into
the bowl, I think about how much I'll miss my routine.
Though I want to be out doing all the things Alex and I
discussed, after such a long time spent going through the

same motions, I'll miss the consistency that Joey provides. I go to grab the Saran Wrap out of the drawer in our island when I see Joey sitting on the couch with his laptop. The lights that are on only illuminate the hallway and the kitchen, so he appears as a dark shadow. I thought that he was upstairs.

I walk over to him and place my hand on his shoulder.

"Honey, are you okay?" I ask.

As I peer down towards his laptop, I shoot my arm back to my side. He's watching security footage from the camera outside of the front door. My heart drops.

"Come sit, there's something I want to show you," he says, pulling me onto his lap. Everything inside of me tells me to get up and run. I don't know what he's doing, but something horrifying stirs in my stomach.

"What's going on? Is there someone outside?" I ask.

"Just watch," he says.

He presses play on the computer screen. The date and time rolling in the top left corner is from last spring. I watch as I enter the frame, and someone follows behind me. It's Fallon. It's the night of Dan and Alex's engagement party. I gasp knowing that he's watched this video. He knows that I had another man in our home. His grip tightens around my knee, pressing his thumbs into my skin: It hurts. Watching this with him hurts more. I watch as Fallon kisses me. I watch as I refuse to stop him. I watch as I lead him into the doorway of our home. I know what happens next and I'm sure Joey knows what happens too. I close the laptop and turn to him.

"Joey, I'm so sorry," I beg, knowing that it's too late; whatever comes next has already been decided.

He pushes me off of him and grabs a fistful of my hair, dragging me into the kitchen. My mind is blank and my cries turn into shrieks. He pushes me up against the fridge by the sides of my throat. He squeezes so tightly that it's enough for me to question whether or not this is the moment he kills me. He grabs the sides of my cheeks, pressing into them again.

"I hate you!" he screams at me.

"Joe-," I try to let out. "Please... stop." I don't know if he can understand me.

"Shut the fuck up," he says knocking my head back into the fridge.

He then backs away from me for a moment. He continues speaking as if he doesn't realize what he's doing. As if he thinks we're just simply arguing back and forth. I feel along my scalp to find there's blood dripping from where he pulled. In the living room I can see chunks of my hair along the floor.

"It's that guy in Dan's wedding party," he says, his voice lowering the more he speaks. It scares me more when he stops yelling. "I recognized him the moment I saw him. I talked to him tonight. I asked him how he knew you and he said he met you the night he drove you home from Alex's party. The son of a bitch couldn't even look me in my eye."

His words don't fully stick with me. I can hardly breathe. I've slumped down to the floor by the fridge. My hands are by my side because it's too painful to place them anywhere else.

"Get up," he demands. It takes me a moment, but I comply. "We're leaving tomorrow to go to the States. They need me to start my job earlier and I think you need to start over too."

"I can't," I cry.

He has taken everything away from me. If I seclude myself even more than I already have, he'll kill me. I don't doubt for a moment that another day spent in this house will cost me my life.

"Don't you dare talk back to me after the shit you pulled," he says.

"Why are you doing this?" I plead. "If you want to hurt me, just do it. I can't do this anymore!"

With that he turns, and his fist comes at my face. I'm now lying on the ground and I can see blood running down into the cracks of the kitchen floor. I must have hit something on my way down, but I can't remember.

I watch as he walks away from me, leaving me alone. He turns the light out and I'm struggling to stay awake. I'm trying to keep quiet, but my whimpers won't stop coming. I think I'm dying. It feels as though I am. I only needed one more night and I could have been free.

Chapter Seventeen

the day of the wedding...

My head is cold and my eyes are sore. As I become more and more aware of where I am, I realize that every part of my body is sore too. I move my arms and lift my head off of the floor. It's heavy and sticky from the blood which is trailing around the corner of our island and fading behind it. I know that I'm in my kitchen but I can't remember how I got here. I go to open my mouth, but I can't speak. My throat is too dry.

I pull myself to sit upright and I can hear voices that feel faded out rapidly grow louder with each second that passes. Quiet talking turns to screaming. It pierces the parts of my body that are already aching. How is it that I can't remember a single thing?

"Why don't you just let us see her?" one of the voices say.

"Please, Joey. Let us get her some help," another adds. I realize that the voices are speaking to Joey. I can see him pacing around in front of me, stuck so far in his own head that he doesn't see me as I inch forward.

"Just leave!" I hear him shout. "Get the fuck out of my house!"

His hands are grabbing at his hair and he's sighing deeply, trying to force himself to breathe.

"Come on, man. Don't be like this. At least let me see if she's alive," I hear the voice break into a sob.

In the distance I see Alex. She hasn't looked at me. She turns to walk out of the house with her phone pressed to her ear. I assume that the man must be Dan.

I bring myself around the corner but Joey steps in front of me, stopping me from going any further.

"Josie, thank god!" Dan gasps. "Don't worry; the police are on their way. Alex and I are going to get you to the hospital. Joey won't let me near you so just hold on, okay?" he says as he cries.

I sit back, trying to focus on what's happening in front of me. My head feels heavy and I feel out of breath. Each time I touch the back of my head I cringe. It hurts so badly. I want Alex to come inside and sit with me. I want someone to hold me.

I start thinking about the last thing I did before I went to sleep. I suddenly remember the videos. Joey found out about Fallon. *Fallon.* God, I wonder if he's okay. I don't know how long I've been lying here, but by the trail of blood hardened from the living room to where I was laying in the kitchen, it must have been hours. Alex runs back into the room frantically. She holds Dan. I can tell that she's petrified. I want to tell her to go, that she doesn't need to stay here and see this, but I'm scared that once she leaves Dan will too, and I'll be alone with him again.

"Dan, they're on their way," she says gripping her cellphone tightly in her hands.

"Just let us take her," Dan begs again.

"We should have come last night. She was going to leave you," Alex says.

Her words are shaking Joey. When I scream for him to stop, he never does. When anyone else sheds light on who he is, he scatters. He doesn't know how to compose himself.

"She's coming with me. We're leaving today," he snaps.

"Coming where?" Dan says with worry.

"To America. This is all her fault. If she wasn't such a whore, I would have never done this. You think I wanted this? If she didn't sleep with your friend Fallon, this wouldn't have happened," Joey rambles.

"You're fucking insane. Do you not remember sleeping with my sister? Or how about the nurse at your hospital? You're pathetic. At least Fallon actually loves her. That's probably why he did it. Where were you when she needed someone to drive her home, or on her birthday?" Alex says getting closer to him.

This sets Dan off. He tells her to go upstairs and pack something for me. I don't think she can stand to see me like this. I'm now sitting against the island behind Joey. He hasn't touched me since I woke up. I'm so glad that Dan's here, but I'm scared about how irrational he's is making Joey. I think that he really thought he could do this to me and proceed to take me out of the country. I've never seen him as out of control as he is right now. That thought in itself is petrifying. I see him reach into his back pocket. He has a switchblade. I can tell by the yellow top of it. I recognize it as the one we use to cut boxes in the garage. This makes me tense. I don't know how long Alex and Dan have been here. I don't even know what time it is. I'm scared to get in front of a mirror to see how much damage he's done. I just want to run as far as I can away from this situation. That thought quickly fades from my mind as I don't even have the strength to stand up at this moment. I don't think that he would use a knife on me. At this point, I don't even feel like I know him at all to tell what he would and wouldn't do.

I can see him feeling around in his pocket. He grabs the end of the switchblade and pulls. I can't let this happen. I swing my arm around and grab his leg, trying to pull him. He hardly flinches. I don't know why I thought I would be strong enough to hurt him; I'm not even strong enough when I'm not all bruised and battered. He quickly whips the blade open and crunches down to my level. He points the blade in my face.

"You better watch it. Not another peep from you until we leave. Got it? Or do I need to show you how sharp this thing is?" he says.

He leans in to grab me and I flinch, but before he can get a hold of me, I see Dan tackle him onto the ground. He's trying to grab the blade from Joey. I see the blade slide onto the floor and a line of blood flies with it. I'm not sure who is bleeding. They struggle for a minute until Joey has barely overtaken Dan. I can see the fear in Dan's eyes. I sit beside them frozen. My first attempt at stopping Joey almost resulted in a knife to my face. I can see the blood coming from Dan's right arm; it isn't a big cut, but it looks deep. He isn't fazed by that at all. His only focus is on gaining control back. I see Joey reaching for the knife while trying to keep Dan pinned down. That's when the police come rushing in, breaking the two apart. They call for backup and take the guys to opposite ends of the room. More and more officers come rushing in.

In this moment I feel like it's okay to let go. I've been using all of my strength to stay upright so I let myself lay back down. The paramedics come rushing in. They ask me a few questions before moving me onto a stretcher, but I can't hear what they're saying. The realization of everything that's just unfolded is too overwhelming. All I can think about is how my life as I once knew it is over. This is not the way I wanted it to end.

I see the police officers placing Joey under arrest putting handcuffs on him. He looks at me as I leave. His eyes tell me that I'm dead to him. It's probably better this way. I hear the officer talking to Dan call over another paramedic to look at his arm but Dan says he doesn't need one and that they should focus on me.

Alex rushes down the stairs and follows us out of the house as the paramedics load me into the ambulance.

"Can I come with her?" she asks.

"Yes, come on in," the paramedic says.

"Alex, you should go. You need to get ready for the wedding," I let out. These are the first words I've said all morning.

"You're getting married?" the paramedic says.

"Yeah, but that can wait," she answers.

"Congratulations," he says.

"Thanks," she says back, trying not to cry. "Josie, I'm going to cancel the wedding if you can't be there. I'm sure Dan will agree. Let's talk more about it later," she suggests.

"Will I be able to go?" I ask.

"Let's see what the doctors say," Alex says before the paramedic can answer.

The paramedic begins asking medical questions. Alex has my wallet with all of my information in it and responds for me. They do some tests on me while she answers most of the questions and they give me something for my pain. My eyes follow Alex's hair as she twirls it around nervously in her fingers. She looks back and forth between the paramedic and I, sending me smiles between words. As the ambulance pulls up to the hospital Alex pulls me close and whispers in my ear.

"Even though this isn't the way we planned it, you did it. You've made it out alive and I'm so proud of you."

--

We've been at the hospital for a few hours now. I didn't have to wait in any crazy lines like I normally do when I come here. I guess it's because I don't normally arrive in an ambulance. The doctor has stitched the side of my arm and the back of my head. He tells me that most of the blood came from my arm and that the cut must have reopened from Joey grabbing me so hard. He explains that I should be expecting some bruising on my face from where he hit me. He also tells me that I'm lucky to be alive. Now that a doctor has looked at my injuries, I can confidently say that I'm going to be okay. This thought makes me cry softly. The memory of last night's events is something I may never get over, but I can finally express the emotions that I have been holding in for the last few years. I'm thankful that I can put Joey behind me, yet I'm worried about my future alone and I'm also worried about the wedding. The doctor tells me that after being awake for so long and not needing any sort of surgery or serious medication besides pain killers and stitches, I should be fine to go to the wedding as long as I don't stay there for too long and don't drink any alcohol.

Alex comes into the room after the doctor leaves. She gives me a huge hug and kisses my head. She tells me that Dan's fine, and he'll be ready to go after he gets a few stitches on his arm.

"We'll be matching," I joke. Alex lets out a half-smile.

"I spoke with the doctor and he told me that you can still come to the wedding, but I don't know if that's such a good idea. We have a lot to figure out and I don't know what's going on with Joey. I'm worried about if he's released and finds the location of the reception," she says with concern. "I want to feel confident that you're safe. I know I'll be distracted, and I need to know that there's someone watching over you."

"Al, I'm coming. I know that I've been getting in the way of every aspect of your wedding, but if there's still enough time to have it, I would love to be there," I say, holding her hand. "I just need a few hours to rest and I promise I'll be okay to come. I just hate the fact that when you think of your wedding day, you'll also think about what Joey did to me."

"No matter how much you disagree, none of this was your fault. You're a strong woman Josephine, and there's nobody I'd rather have beside me," she says, comforting me. "The wedding planner said that we can push it back until 8:00p.m. so Dan and I would probably have to go soon and get ready. The doctor told us that there are some police officers here to talk to you now but I don't want you to be here alone."

"I honestly feel much safer now than I have in the past year. Although I am a complete mess, I'm okay. At least, I know I'm going to be. I've got this," I reply.

"I know you do. I just wanted to hear you say it. I can get my sister to pick you up if you want," she suggests.

"I can't go with Jessica," I say quickly. "Last time I saw her she tried to fight me and she kind of has an advantage on me now that I'm all bruised up."

"No, not her; Emily. She said she can stop by if you wanted to go," she clarifies.

"Yeah, that would be great," I say.

I can't be too picky right now. I'm nervous for people to see me like this. I don't want to tell people about what happened but I don't want to lie either. Alex leaves the room and two officers enter, sitting down on either side of me.

"How are you feeling, Josephine?" the female officer says.

"I'm okay," I say shyly, my hands are shaking.

"We're sorry to hear what happened this morning. We're glad to see you here alive though. Far too often in situations like these we don't get to meet the victims of spousal abuse. We're going to be the ones dealing with your case. I'm Officer James and my colleague here is Officer Hillard," the male officer says.

"It's nice to meet you," I respond.

"We need to ask you a few questions about what happened today. Is there anything that you want to ask us before we start?" Officer Hillard asks.

I sit for a moment before I reply, "yes, I just wanted to know how Joey's doing?" The looks on their faces show that they're surprised by my concern for him. I don't know why I care either. I just know that he must be feeling lost too.

"Joey's going to be spending a bit of time at the station today. Then once he gets a court date, it will determine whether or not he goes to jail. We can also look into a restraining order, whatever you're comfortable with," Officer James says.

"In regard to how he's doing mentally, he seems to be okay. It's hard to say; we weren't the officers dealing with him today. I would try not to worry so much about that," Officer Hillard says. She gives me a warm smile. I feel comfortable with her.

We go back and forth about my relationship with Joey. We talk a lot about last night and the events leading up to when the police arrived. I can't remember a lot of what happened before he hit me. I just remember him hitting me hard in the face and waking up to Dan and Alex being there. I tell them about our entire relationship and that in the past few months he had been cheating on me regularly. I also admit to them that I've been sleeping with someone too. I tell them about the times where he pushed me down the stairs, and when he would grab me forcefully. I tell them about the years before that; the good years. I tell them about the times where I felt like I knew him.

Particularly, I talk them through our trip to France when we first met. That was the best trip of my life. It was when he was still trying to win me over. I wasn't ready to be in a relationship but he used his money and charm to make me ready. In his sister's eyes I was the perfect person to settle him down; an opinion that unfortunately changed over the years. That trip lasted fourteen days. Each day I woke up in a white room with the wind blowing over the balcony and into our bed. I would open my eyes to soft hands trailing my skin, and blue eyes that would water at the idea of having met me. He seemed so soft and pure; I couldn't help but fall in love with him. We would spend our afternoons shopping and eating sandwiches at cafes lining streets with soft music rolling through our ears. He would make me try things on for him in boutiques and we would taste fresh chocolate in small shops. We ate dinner under the Eiffel tower and we danced in the streets. The man I saw today was not the man I fell in love with. This version of him might have been there all along. I'm not so sure anymore.

At the end of my story I begin to cry hysterically. So much so that the nurse is called in to touch up a stitch on my head. Officer James and Officer Hillard decide that it's probably best if we have the rest of our interview once I've had a bit of time to process everything. They tell me to call them if I have any important information to tell them, or if I feel ready to talk before they contact me. I shake their hands and they leave.

Now that I'm completely alone, I let out a deep breath. I haven't stopped crying all morning, even though I feel like there are no tears left inside of me to cry out. I know I should probably stay home tonight, but I feel like I need to be there for Alex. I don't think staying home will make me feel any safer or any happier.

I lay my head back into the pillow and look out the window beside me. The sky is lined baby blue today and the clouds rest softly without a care in the world. I feel broken inside and wish desperately to feel as the sky does in this moment. I wish that God will give me the strength to make it through another night, for Alex.

Chapter Eighteen

A few hours after the police leave, I receive a text from Emily; she's going to be downstairs in ten minutes. I get up from the bed where I've been napping and walk over to the bathroom so I can begin to get ready. I've learned to cover bruises and light cuts with makeup, but I've never had to cover up stitches. My doctor told me to let them breathe, and I'm scared to infect them, so I leave the cuts visible. The most I can take is a lightly tinted moisturiser over the bruising. I can already see the black and blue spots forming on the left side of my face. I unzip the backpack that Alex brought me before she left. She told me she went back to the house to get some things for me once the doctors told us that I'd be able to go to the wedding. She packed my bridesmaids dress at the top of the bag along with a tracksuit underneath. I slip on my dress and look in the mirror. I look like a mess and the thought of people seeing me today is making me anxious.

Alex brought over a hair curler and some makeup, but I feel as though I should be doing this kind of stuff for her today.

I do my hair, letting it hang loose, just a few pins to hold it in place. I keep my makeup simple: blush pink lines my lips and coats my eyes. I do my best to cover the bruises with powder and concealer, but they still show through underneath. I strap my heels on and gather my things, trying not to catch my reflection as I walk around the room.

The nurse walks in and she stumbles when she looks at me, almost as if she doesn't recognize me. It makes me laugh a bit.

"Wow, Mrs. Parker you look amazing!" she says with a smile.

"Thank you," I say back.

"Are you ready to go now? Are you sure you don't want to rest a while longer?" she asks.

"No, I have to be at a wedding. Maid of honour," I say pointing at myself. She nods and helps me with my things.

"Let me walk you downstairs; I want to make sure you make it out okay," she insists.

I feel like everyone I've met today has sugar coated each word they've said to me as if I'm some broken little flower that can't stand upright. Yes, I may have broken down, but one night of abuse doesn't hold a candle to the last year I've endured. I'm stronger than they think. Stares follow me as I walk down the hallways. The nurse and I make small talk about the wedding. I practice tip toeing around the topic of Joey with her and it isn't as hard as I imagined. However, this nurse doesn't know me. She must see people like me all the time. We reach the pickup area of the hospital. She gives me a hug and I wonder if she does that for everyone. It's nice, nonetheless. Every touch I get helps me replace the fear Joey has instilled in me. I turn back around and see Emily pull up in her car.

"Hey, hon," Emily says softly as she rolls down her window.

"Hey, Em," I say opening the door and giving her a hug. Alex took most of my stuff with her in Dan's car when she left so that I didn't have to carry anything.

"I'm glad we get some time before the wedding. I don't know if you want to talk about it, but I'm here if you decide to. I promised Alex and Dan that I would take care of you tonight," she says lightly. I'm glad that she's not being awkward about Joey or about what happened with her sister.

"Maybe we can just listen to the radio. At least, for now," I suggest.

She turns the radio up just loud enough to block out the hum of the car's tires turning on the gravel beneath us. The drive is cut in half since we're not taking the back roads and the hospital is along the highway. I lean my head against the window and drift off for a while. I never usually fall asleep in cars unless I've drank too much. I probably haven't felt this relaxed in a long time. It was most likely Joey that kept me awake. Things with Joey fell apart so quickly; once the light shone on all of his flaws, I couldn't help but notice them. He became like an ant under a magnifying glass and things became too heated for him to stand still any longer.

We pull up to the wedding and the parking lot is full of cars. There isn't any movement outside. Everyone must already be inside, waiting for me. I feel guilty because nobody knew the wedding would fall behind by three hours. Everyone must be starving, and I think about how rumors spread like wildfire in Alex's family. They'll all know the delay for the wedding was my fault.

There are almost no parking spots left so we park the car at the end of the lot.

"Are you ready?" she asks, turning to look at me.

"Not really, but I have to be," I almost whisper back.

"That's my girl," she says hugging me again.

We take our things and head to Alex's room. The halls are clear. Everyone must be in the dining hall and bar.

Emily tells me that they moved dinner up to before the wedding to accommodate me. It's one of those things that Alex did because she's an amazing friend. It makes me feel bad about our argument the other day.

We get to her room and knock on the door. Alex sings a huge hello and her sister Jessica opens the door.

"Welcome," she says with a smile. I hope she was too drunk to remember that she tried to fight me last night, and I hope she's drunk enough now not to care. Alex is sitting getting her hair done and it looks like it's almost finished.

"Alex, you look beautiful!" I say loudly from the doorway. I walk up to her and kiss her cheek. The lady doing her hair asks me not to do that again as she's already had her makeup done.

"Says you," Alex replies, looking over at my dress. I've done a decent job at hiding the bruises. The only cut you can see is on my forearm, matching Dan's.

The girls are drinking mimosas and opening small gifts that Alex bought for us. They're small diamond necklaces that look just like the earrings Alex and I bought on that trip to New York for her birthday.

"Try it on!" she says handing me a box.

I open the box and put it on. She pulls her hair behind her ear and shows me her earrings.

"I bought them to match," she says confirming my thoughts.

She passes me a pouch and asks me to open it, inside are my earrings. She wants me to match with her. My heart overflows.

"Alex," I say hugging her, trying not to cry.

"I swiped them off of your nightstand. I wanted to match with my best friend," she says lovingly.

She walks back over to get the final touches of her hair done. She then walks in the closet to put on her gown. When she comes out, we all gasp. I cried when she tried it on for the first time but seeing it all together on her wedding day takes my breath away. I'm so proud of her.

"I said this on the day that you bought your dress: your mom would be so proud of you," I watch her twirl around in excitement.

"Thanks, babe," she says to me. I know Alex is sad that her mom can't be here with her today. I can feel it in my heart that she's in the room with us though, smiling and crying right beside her. Once the commotion of her reveal winds down I decide it's time I sneak off to find the groom.

"Do you mind if I go see Dan before the ceremony? I ask her.

"No, not at all. I think he's getting ready still in room 230 by the lobby," she says.

I leave the room and head to the bar. I want to bring him a shot to cheers him before he goes out there. Dan did the same thing for me on my wedding day. It's our tradition now. I make a promise to myself that this will be the one and only thing I drink tonight. I get to the bar which isn't far from the lobby. It's close enough for me to grab a quick drink without anyone coming up to me.

I slide in between two seats and try to wave the bartender down. It takes him a minute to notice. As I wait, I turn down the bar to see if anyone is looking at me. I see Jessica and Fallon directly across from me. I guess she left the room when I did. I don't know what they're talking about, but she seems stressed. Her arms are waving up and down and she has a line between her eyebrows showing signs of distress. Fallon has his hand on her shoulder. I see him mouth the words "calm down" a few times, then he leans in and kisses her cheek. That's when his eyes meet mine and I turn away quickly.

"Two shots of tequila," I say sliding ten dollars in the bartender's direction.

"Coming right up," the bartender replies.

I feel a tap on my shoulder and as I turn, I'm met by Fallon's eyes. It looks like he's been crying, it's a look I recognize from the night we met.

He hugs me without saying a word. I can feel everything he wants to tell me through how he's holding me in his arms.

He then whispers into my ear, "I'm sorry." I know that he's referring to ignoring me last night and to what happened today with Joey.

I pull away from him and look up to see a tear sliding down his face.

"I don't have time to talk right now, Fallon," I reply softly. I feel bad acting cold towards him, but I am still upset that he told Alex about the abuse with Joey. I understand now that he did it to protect me, but it felt like a violation of trust. I don't have the time to sit and dissect our relationship right now. "Sorry, I just have to go see Dan before the wedding starts."

"Don't worry, I'll be around. I'm just glad you came today," he says before turning to walk back to Jessica.

I turn back to face the bar and wait for my drinks. I hate tequila, but it's Dan's favourite. At my wedding Dan brought me rum. Dan hates rum and he drank it for me so I think I owe him the same courtesy. The bartender slides the drinks over to me and I turn to leave without looking back. I walk as fast as I can to room 230 and use my foot to knock on the door once I arrive.

The door cracks open and I slip in. Dan greets me with a hug and takes a drink from my hand.

"I knew you wouldn't forget," he says smiling at me, "thanks."

"I didn't want to let you down. How are you feeling? Nervous?" I ask.

"Not anymore," he laughs. "How are you feeling? Let me know if you need anything today, OK?"

"I think I'm okay, I don't really know. I'm trying not to think too much about it," I reply.

He nods, showing he understands. We lift our glasses together and shoot the shots back.

Once we're finished, I turn and see Mark and Charlie in the room. I didn't expect Charlie to be here and I don't understand why he is; Jade just had their baby only days ago. I can hardly look at him.

"Holy shit, you look rough," Charlie says with a laugh.

"Shut up, Charlie. If I hear another word about it, you can leave," Dan snaps. "Sorry, Josie. You know that guy's an idiot."

I nod and take a step toward the door. I'm trying not to let his words affect me. I'm sure I'll get a lot of comments like this one throughout the night so I need to prepare myself.

"Good luck out there, Dan. Knock em' dead," I say as I leave the room.

My walk back to Alex's room is long. I get lost a few times along the way, asking numerous people to point me in the right direction. I think after all that's happened today my mind is scattered. I get to the room and all of the girls are ready to go. It's time to make Alex a bride.

We walk out the doors to a deserted hallway. We pass the bar and see that it's cleared out. I hold Alex's hand as we walk down the hall, telling her over and over again how beautiful she is. She knows it though; I don't have to tell her. I can feel her nervousness stir as we approach the doors to the ceremony. Someone signals that we're here and we get in formation. I'm still holding Alex's hand.

"You've got this," I say to her.

"Thanks, Jos. I couldn't do this without you. Thank you for being brave for me," she says.

The music starts and the doors swing open. Hundreds of eyes fall in our direction. I can feel people trying to look past Emily, Jessica, and Abigail at me. The last thing I wanted was Alex's wedding day to be about anything other than her. The thing about Alex is that she would rather me be here and have all of the attention than me not be here at all. She's grown into such a beautiful woman; she wasn't like this when I met her and I'm so happy I got to be here to see that change.

287

Chapter Nineteen

The girls file out one at a time. I can tell Abigail has been working on her walk. It's my turn to go and I force my feet to move. I focus on my steps and I don't look at a single person other than Dan as I walk up the aisle. It looks so beautiful in here and I know Alex must be thrilled with how it turned out. There are white and pale pink flowers lining every inch of this room and candles all along the outsides of the aisle. Her dream has come true. As I get to Dan, he grazes my arm; I know how happy he is that I'm here.

I can feel everyone's eyes on me even as Alex takes her turn to walk down the aisle. I'm subject to everyone's curiosity. I choose to stare at Alex, she deserves at least two sets of eyes on her tonight; mine and Dan's. She's absolutely stunning. She's wearing the perfect dress and is marrying the perfect man. As she walks closer Dan loses it; he's crying tears for her. They've come so far and I know that he sees it as he looks at her.

"You look incredible, baby," he says, kissing her hand as she reaches him.

The crowd lets out an "awww" as she leans over to wipe his tears. The ceremony begins and they try hard to get the words right. I laugh because I know they chose the shortest vows possible; they both just want to get to the partying. They know how much they care for each other. They don't care about the words in between it all. I look past Dan and my eyes meet Fallon's. He was already looking at me. I can see compassion and hurt in his eyes. I think about how he would make the perfect husband if he were willing to put down his walls. It's heart wrenching because I feel that we have what Dan and Alex have. I wish that it could have been Fallon and I saying these words to each other, but it isn't.

Dan turns to Fallon and he breaks his eye contact with me. He hands Dan the ring and I take that as my cue to get Alex's ring ready for her. They slide the rings onto each other's hands and repeat after the officiant, then embrace in a kiss that strings on for a few seconds. The crowd is cheering wildly. Alex and Dan hold each other's faces for a moment, both in awe. The officiant announces that they're husband and wife and they begin back down the aisle. We all follow suit.

Fallon reaches out proudly this time to take my arm and guides me down the aisle. He holds it silently and it feels like he actually wants to be holding me. He has his free hand resting over top of my arm. I feel him letting me know that he can feel my pain. Joey's nowhere in sight and as uncomfortable as it is to have all of these eyes on me, I feel okay. I feel safe and secure, even if only for a moment.

"I'm proud of you," Fallon whispers in my ear as we come to the end of the aisle. I look up at him and smile sadly.

I see Jessica run up and grab his other arm, pulling him from me.

"Come on, I want you to meet my mom," she says taking him away.

I follow Alex and Dan into the reception room as everyone takes their seats. The music starts and everyone gets back up. Traditionally, people have dinner after the ceremony but since dinner was already served, it's now time for the first dance. We all gather in a circle in the middle of the room as Alex and Dan cross past us and take center stage. Their song comes on over the speakers; a song they heard the night they met at the bar. I watch as Alex's head falls onto Dan's shoulder. His hand is on the back of her head pulling her in. They are so in love that they don't care who's watching them; they just long to be close to one another. I realize right in this moment that leaving Joey was the right thing to do. I don't want to waste my time in fear of getting hurt and miss out on finding the person who I can have a moment like this with.

As the song gets close to its end the other couples from the wedding party begin to join in. There will be another slow song playing immediately following the first dance. I see Mark and Emily take the floor, then Abigail and Jack, followed by Fallon and Jessica. I walk over to my seat and watch them intently from a distance. Jessica's so into him it makes me sad. I watch her staring at him and he's looking everywhere else but at her. I don't understand why he chooses to date these girls that he won't be with for longer than a week. He picks the same blonde, short, blue eyed girls over and over again.

Abigail and Jack break apart from the dance as more people begin to join in. They head over to me and ask how I'm doing. Jack asks me where Joey is and I realize that they have no clue about what happened. I anticipated this question being asked but I do not yet have a valid answer other than the truth.

"He's moved to America for work," I say. That's all I can think of in the moment. It's true but it just probably isn't going to happen for a while now.

"Oh, it's strange that he left today of all days. He told me he was looking forward to the wedding. He also said you were moving to the States with him," Jack says with confusion.

"Yeah, things changed," I say flatly.

"Did you get into a car accident or something? Those bruises look horrible," Abigail says.

I'm not sure if she's trying to be a bitch or if this is really how she talks to people. First Charlie, now her. I guess I'm getting all of the bad ones over with first.

"Nope," I say. "I kind of have a headache, would you mind if I just sit here by myself for a minute?" I ask.

"No, not at all. Sorry if we bugged you," Jack says. I don't know how such a nice guy like him ended up with Abigail.

I watch as Fallon makes his way over to the bar. Jessica's arms begin to move in a craze around her as they were earlier, she must be pissed at Fallon again. Alex told me that Fallon only drinks on the anniversary of his parent's death but he seems to be drinking far more often these days.

I continue to watch Jessica's meltdown as Mark and Emily approach me. I'm not in the mood to hide my feelings about Jessica anymore. I don't like her. I think that being single at a wedding really brings out the worst in people.

"They've been arguing all night," Emily says as she sits down beside me.

"I can see that," I sigh. "I wish I could have a drink. I don't know how I'll survive the night without one, looking like this."

"Trust me Josephine, give yourself time. All of that will heal and you'll find the person for you. He might even be in this room," Mark says lightly.

"Maybe," I say, pouring water from the pitcher into a cup and taking a sip.

"Do you know where you're going to be staying after all of this?" Mark asks.

"No, not a clue. Probably at Alex's place. She and Dan are going on their honeymoon right after this. Their place will be a ghost town," I say.

I have thought about staying with my mom, but I bet that Joey's already tried calling her. I need to be away from all of that for now.

"Do you not have to work?" Emily asks.

"Actually, I don't work. Joey didn't let me," I say. It feels good to finally let go of the lies.

"Are you going to get out and dance?" Mark asks lightly. I think he realizes that all of the questions are starting to make me uncomfortable.

"Probably not. The closer I stay to my seat, the less of a chance I have to run into people who want to pry. I can't handle another bad reaction from people," I answer.

"I'm sorry people are so nosy," Emily sighs.

"I knew what I was getting myself into by coming today," I say.

"Let us know if we can do anything for you at all. You can even stay with me if Alex won't take you, but I know she will. I just want you to know that you have options," she adds.

I smile at her and they walk off. I sit back in my chair and think some more about Fallon. The more he ignores me the more it drives me insane. One minute he's telling me he's proud of me, and the next he's dancing with Alex's sister. He probably doesn't even care. The more I think of starting over the more scared I become. When I spoke with Alex about dating and my future I was thinking about Fallon, even though I told myself I wasn't. I just didn't want the reason I left Joey to be about another man. It was so much more than that.

It's extremely difficult to ignore him and it's even more difficult knowing that tonight will probably be the last I see of him. Unless he marries Jessica. God, I hope that doesn't happen. I don't think I could bear it as he's in and out of every breath I've taken in the past year. It took me five years to forget about him the first time, how long will it take for me to get over him a second time? If I can't have a future with him, I don't know if I'll be able to have one with anyone else. I'm really questioning if it's too late to move from one life and onto the next one.

--

I decide that I need to get something to eat. I thought that I could hold off, but I think I'll go crazy if I sit here for another second without food. I get up and walk over to the buffet around the corner from the reception. There are bits and pieces of food everywhere; the damage has already been done. I haven't eaten all day and I think I'll faint if I don't get something in me. Alex sees me and comes over; I can tell she's a little drunk.

"Hey, Josie, come here!" she points at me and waves me over as if she has to tell me a secret.

"Alex, what are you doing?" I ask with a laugh.

"Follow me," she says as she prances off and down the hallway. We get to the doorway of her room and she opens it. There's a tray of covered food waiting. "Let's eat, I'm starving."

We dive into a plate of McDonald's burgers and fries. She must have just had it ordered because it's still warm.

"Don't forget your evening medication. The doctor said you need to take it with food," she says pointing to the bag she packed me.

"I love you, Alex," I say. She's so kind.

I take a painkiller and start to eat. She has a bottle of non-alcoholic champagne tucked under the table and it's already opened. We share it back and forth until it's halfway empty. She begins to tell me about the fight between Fallon and Jessica. She knows that I don't want to talk about Joey. At least not tonight.

"She wouldn't stop crying after the ceremony. She hates your guts because Fallon wouldn't stop staring at you," she says.

I can tell how drunk she is by the way she's speaking. It's hysterical.

"I saw them fighting before the ceremony so it couldn't have been all about me," I say.

"It's probably not," she says giggling as she shoves fries into her mouth. "But I do know a secret."

"What is it?" I ask.

"I think now that you're single again you should date Fallon," she says.

"Fallon's dating your sister," I correct.

"No, he's not. They were never dating. Besides, she just left the wedding crying about him with Emily. It was crazy," she adds.

"I feel badly for her," I say. I'm trying to be sensitive to the fact that Jessica is her sister. Truthfully, I couldn't care less if she were here or not.

"I don't. I'm pretty sure he's in love with you," she says. "People who love each other should be together."

"I don't love him," I say, although I've already admitted to myself that I do.

"You're not fooling anyone," she says. "I see the way you two go googly-eyed at each other any time you're in the same room. It's disgusting. It's worse than Dan and I."

"Whatever you say, boss," I reply. "We should probably head back now."

"You're right, my husband might be off looking for me," she says.

I know that she's probably right about Fallon and I. We do love each other in an unexplainable way, but timing has never been on our side. I don't think that anyone would want to be brought into this mess that I've made with Joey. I know I wouldn't want to be. The more that I think about it, the more I realize that I'm so willing to move on because what I had with Joey ended years ago. It ended the first time he cheated on me. It was something that I couldn't get over. Maybe Joey and I never had a chance to begin with. I knew that the moment I saw Fallon he would be a part of me forever. I wasn't quite sure how back then. It seems now that he might be the part of me that I can never have. I don't think he will want someone who is so broken.

Alex and I get up off of the couch and put our shoes back on. Before we go to exit the door, she turns to me.

"Josie, can you promise me something? Actually, two things," she asks.

"Sure, anything," I say looking at her.

"First you have to promise you won't ever lie to me again," she says. I know very well that she's talking about Joey. I feel horrible for lying to her for him. She's one of the only people I've ever been honest with. She knows what I need more than I do sometimes.

"Of course," I say.

"Good. And second, you have to talk to Fallon tonight. Just make sure he's okay," she says.

Because she's the bride, I agree, and we walk out of the room.

Chapter Twenty

I walk back to the reception with Alex after our secret meal and begin to head over to the bar to grab a drink: non-alcoholic, unfortunately. I order a water and head over to the window, watching as Alex walks back over to Dan. He hasn't been off of the dance floor all night. I watch as the song changes to a sad one; some song about falling in love and never letting go of it. Dan holds the small of Alex's back and whispers something to her. She laughs and kisses him. I can see his eyes water from happiness all the way over here. I know that for them, the feelings they share now will last a lifetime. There aren't a lot of men in this world like Dan. Alex is a lucky woman. And Dan is a lucky man.

I glance out the window to the back patio. The details of this wedding are stunning. I love it more now than I did when Alex and I picked all of it. Through the window I can see Fallon sitting on a bench by himself. I feel an urge to go talk to him because I haven't spoken to him all night. He looks defeated and I decide that it's time to fulfil my promise to Alex, so I begin to walk outside toward him.

I walk up to him and sit up on the bench beside him. We sit quietly for a moment and he doesn't move. He didn't watch me walk over and he didn't even flinch as I sat down. I don't know if he's upset with me or not. He's been communicating with me all night through his eyes, disappointment and devastation written all over his face.

"Are you okay?" I ask.

"No, I'm not," he says. "I'm sorry I let this happen to you." I quickly realize that I mistook his disappointment for anger. Not anger pointed in my direction, or even in Joey's, but at himself.

"This isn't your fault, you know. You need to stop blaming yourself for everything bad that happens in your life. You need to allow yourself to be happy," I say. "Alex told me about what happened to your parents, Fallon. The real story."

He looks at me without emotion. It's a place he can't let himself go. I don't push; I just want him to hear those words coming from someone he actually listens to.

He doesn't say anything, so I continue, "look at me, my life's a mess. Last night I wasn't even sure that I would wake up this morning, but I'm here. I'm choosing to swim because if I stopped, I would drown."

Fallon places his hand on my knee, I can see tears pooling in his eyes. I'm glad to see him cry because it means he feels something. It means he's actually hearing my words.

"You're right, Josephine. You don't know how glad I am to see you here tonight," he says looking down at my hand.

"You can't give up on yourself. This isn't what your parents would have wanted for you. There's so much more of this life for you to live if you'll let yourself experience it," I say putting my hand behind his neck and brushing it with my thumb.

"I know. I've realized that today, actually. Watching the way Dan and Alex love each other, it's all I've ever wanted. I don't know if I'll be able to get there though," he sighs. His words crush me a little.

"Why not?" I say trying to push through the hurt.

"Because I could only ever picture that for myself with you. I'm finally ready to let you in and now it's too late," he says sadly. "I looked at the two of them tonight saying their vows and for the first time since my parents died, I craved a wedding and flowers and stupid cheesy wedding music. All of that actually meant something to me today. I finally felt like I could have happiness like that without my parents here."

"Fallon, it's not too late for any of that," I say.

He looks at me sideways, putting his cup down on the bench beside him and stands in front of me.

"You don't hate me?" he asks, placing one hand on my knee.

"Of course not, I could never hate you. Fallon, I think I'm in love with you," I say without thought. This sense of bravery comes from all that happened last night. I've been hurt in every way possible and I almost lost my life because of it. I'm not willing to let another second go by where I don't feel in control of my own life.

"You already know that the feeling is mutual, Josie," he says pulling me to stand with him. He touches the corner of my eyes, wiping away tears. I haven't told someone that I loved them and meant it for a long time.

"Can we finally dance?" he asks.

"I don't really want to go back in there right now," I say shyly.

"No, right here," he says. The music is perfect; a cheesy love song blasts through the speakers inside. It fades perfectly outside, soft enough for me to hear his heartbeat under his shirt.

We dance and the world stops around us. I feel like I've finally met my soul mate, for the second time. He's finally ready for me and I'm finally ready for him. All

I've wanted was to be loved by him. After all that I've been through, I feel as though I deserve it.

"I've been waiting for this moment for five years, Josephine. I can't let you go again knowing that I could risk the possibility of getting you back. I'm ready to bring you into my life if you'll have me," he says into my hair as he dances with me.

"That's all I've ever wanted, Fallon," I say pulling back. He kisses me softly.

"I'm sorry that it took this much for me to realize that you're strong enough to handle my honesty. The moment I let you go back to him, I realized that I need you," he says.

"I haven't been able to shake you no matter how hard I've tried. It feels like the further I try to push away, the closer you get," I say looking up at him. "Before I make any promises though, I want to know what it is that's been holding you back from being ready."

"Can we talk about that tomorrow?" he asks.

"I want to know right now. I want to start things off right," he's being too venerable with me for me to let this question go unanswered.

"Okay, I'll tell you then. I'm worried that I'm going to put you into a difficult situation though. The reason that I've been pushing you away all this time is because I'm involved in something with Dan and Charlie. Something that not even Alex knows about. If I tell you, you can't tell her. It will kill her. It might even kill any chance of you wanting this moment with me right now," he says nervously.

I stand back from him, cutting our dance short. I've wanted this moment for so long. I've racked my brain for hours trying to figure out this piece of him that he kept so restricted. Now that it's in front of me, I don't know if I'm ready for it. I don't know if I can lie to my best friend. I don't know if I can bear to have the only thing in my life that feels whole fall apart. What could I possibly not know about Dan?

I walk up back up to Fallon and place my hand on his shoulder. I know that what he needs to tell me is something that will probably hurt me, but I don't think I can be shocked by much anymore. I need one night of freedom. One more night that I can control.

"You know what, Fallon? It can wait for tomorrow," I say.

I hold my free hand up for him to grab it. A smile crosses his face as he takes hold of it. And we continue dancing.

Made in the USA
Middletown, DE
24 September 2020